Pink Dice

ELLEN EVERMAN

Pink Dice

Acclaim Press
MORLEY, MISSOURI

Acclaim Press
— *Your Next Great Book* —
P.O. Box 238
Morley, MO 63767
(573) 472-9800
www.acclaimpress.com

Steward & Wise
GRAPHIC DESIGN
Designer: Ellen Sikes
Cover Design: Emily Sikes

Library of Congress has catalogued the hardcover edition as follows:

Everman, Ellen, 1951-
  Pink dice / Ellen Everman.
    p. cm.
  ISBN-13: 978-0-9798802-9-2 (alk. paper)
  ISBN-10: 0-9798802-9-7 (alk. paper)
  1. Girls--Fiction. 2. Murder--Fiction. 3. Nineteen fifties--Fiction. 4. Kentucky, Northern--Fiction. 5. Cincinnati (Ohio)--Fiction. I. Title.

  PS3605.V45P56 2008
  813'.6--dc22

                         2008006298

First Paperback Edition, Printed 2022
ISBN: 978-1-956027-20-4 | 1-956027-20-3

Printed in the United States of America
10 9 8 7 6 5 4 3 2 1

Contents

ACKNOWLEDGEMENTS

Joseph P. Surran, Landon L. Wallingford, Dennis W. Steinbis, my sister, Patricia A. Bannon, Seth Tuska and Douglas Hamilton for their encouragement. Judy Campbell and Natalie Rubenstein for their insights. Doug Sikes and Nadine Roberts for their painstaking assistance. Nathan Gabriel for research assistance. Dennis and my nephew, Christopher Bannon, for all that reading.

DEDICATION

To my loving parents, Nietta and Lawrence Everman,
for giving me a childhood in the country.

Pink Dice

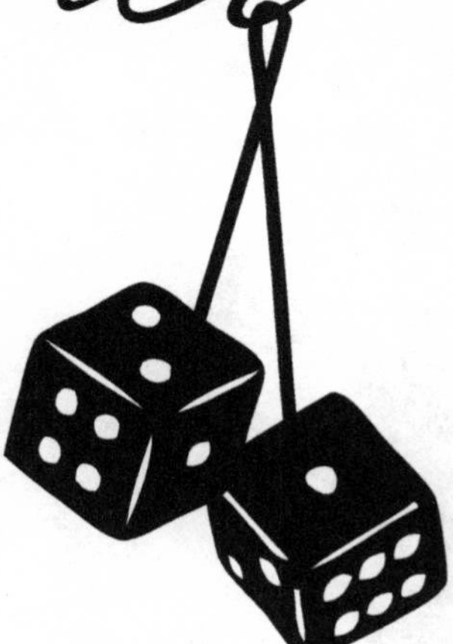

CHAPTER I

Mary Lou

Today we would call Mary Lou drop-dead gorgeous. In the fifties, which is when I remember her best, she was just "beautiful." The pin-curled hairstyle and crinoline-filled dresses made her seem a bit dowdy by today's standards. But certain beauty is as timeless and unmistakable as certain charms. She had that too. Incredible charm. It was as if the gods of good looks, deciding her porcelain-like skin wasn't enough, chose to fill her with some enchanting brew that intoxicates universally. Looking back, it seems they may have given her too much.

I can still see her running into the woods as if it were the only thing that could save her. Her dress is whipping about her legs like the unnamed thing that slows one down in a bad dream. I remember her frightened face, the sick feeling in my stomach. All that beauty and charm. What had gone wrong? It is something I've wondered about through the years, a nagging question never resolved. But I gave it more than the usual passing analysis the other night as I turned over in my mind the events of that long-ago summer. Hoping to find an old photo that might provide some hints, I rummaged through my old cedar chest with a sort of wistful determination.

First thing out was my wedding dress. Dear God. Bittersweet memories. Then Dad's World War II Marine Corps uniform. I smiled to think of him in it. So tall and young. A yellowed issue of Look, the J.F. Kennedy funeral displayed on its front cover, held my attention for a few seconds.

Near the bottom of the heap, I found a small forgotten box labeled "special pictures." The words were written in my own hand…a young and unsure scrawl. I opened the box like a gift. And there it was. Mary Lou just as I remembered her…flashing that winning smile in the old black-and-white photograph Mom took of my cousin and me one bright summer day. For years I suspected this old tattered picture had been lost. I hold it now like an archeological treasure. The shapely vision on the left is Mary Lou. The young girl to her right is me. I'm looking at her, not the camera. It was always that way. I thought her vivid green eyes, her abundantly thick auburn mane and the blush in her cheeks could not be outdone. But mostly I adored her wild anticipation that vanished long ago in the summer air.

"Patti Rae," she instructed me one morning. "Embroidered handkerchiefs are for ladies, you know." How strange that I remember that. Those words were uttered only forty-some years ago and I'm wondering who, in this world, still uses an embroidered handkerchief? But I digress. With that statement, she infused the white linen with a drop of glistening cologne and pushed it deep inside the cleavage of her passionately heaving bosom. She then rushed down the stairs like a wild deer in search of adventure.

My memories become clearer.

He was my closest friend and he understood the hold that Mary Lou had on me. Although a reclusive woodsman and not one to mingle with the crowd, he recognized the enchantress that Mary Lou was. He said it was not just her beauty that attracted. As always and with a gleam in his eyes that I imagined had seen all or most of the world, he hit upon a profound truth: There are many mysteries of nature that pull us toward one person. There are many that repel us from others. But, for me, it was much simpler than that. As an adult, I now see my youthful adoration of Mary Lou was based on one key fact: She was everything I wanted to be.

I followed my wild young cousin down the stairs. My heart rushed ahead of me wanting badly to find out what it was she ran after. Eventually, we would all run after her. My mother, my brother, my father…watching her grab wildly at life before it became vapor in her hands. We were all proud of that unspeakable personality trait, even a bit worshipful of it during those unforgettable hot summer days. Eventually, it frightened us. But the charm remained, and an almost tangible scent of some indistinct prey scampering in the jungle of her dreams kept us in awe and guessing. Her forceful will created an indulgence in my parents I'd not seen before.

One clear, star-lit evening, my mother said to my cousin, "Now Mary Lou, I don't think your mom would like it if she thought you were taking a walk in the woods with a young boy, but…if you promise to be back in twenty minutes…I know you'll be a lady."

My Aunt Elsie would have had a fit. And Mom knew that. But Mom relented mostly because Mary Lou insisted that it was her right as a young adult to do what she pleased.

To be fair, Mary Lou was only reacting to the times. And the times, they weren't just changing. They were transmitting some vast electrical charge through all of us. But only she and, eventually, her generation embraced and acted out the shock.

During this fast-changing period of American history, our Soviet neighbors were busy putting together something that would pierce outer space. So, naturally, we Americans were trying to beat them to it. Car designs took their cues from all the resulting high-tech rocket science. Restless citizens wanted to be part of this fast new order. But the adolescents! Theirs was a more dramatic, more significant change. Suddenly they were no longer expected to act like adults by having babies at age fourteen. Nor was it presumed that poor young boys should work at hard labor as early as twelve or thirteen. FDR and Eleanor had changed all that. Without so much as a blink, this glib new crop of adolescents, with their unprecedented young smarts, understood their advantages and forged a brand new deal with their horizon: No limits. Vain and indomitable, they pulled us, with their music and TV-influenced philosophies, toward their kinder but more chaotic universe. A colorful world of bobby socks, poodle skirts and hip expressions. We called them by their new name: Teenagers.

It was the steamy summer of 1956, and I remember exactly how my cousin looked as if it were yesterday. I was eleven years old going on thirty. Mary Lou was fifteen going on Marilyn Monroe. We hadn't seen her since our last summer visit, three years earlier, to Uncle Robert's modest farm that sprawled chickens, mules, cows and a few tired-out horses just east of

Lexington. It was the year the locusts burst from the earth chattering loudly, riding their brief tide of riotous living. We were surprised to find those three years had made a dramatic difference in Mary Lou's physical appearance and attitude. Gone were the scarlet cheeks radiating perfect health from the strong thrust of a Tomboy's heart. Her boisterous will was now tamed into a coquettish cajoling. We might have expected a different Mary Lou had we considered her formative age.

One evening, two weeks after Mary Lou's arrival, I heard Dad reminiscing about the old Mary Lou and how once her horse, Freckles, had been her entire world. Mom listened intently, understanding Dad's concern. In the dim light, sitting across from each other at the kitchen table, they whispered their private thoughts about Mary Lou as our boathouse windows volleyed yellow beams of light out into the softening coolness of dusk. Mary Lou lay upstairs in a coma-like sleep. They thought I was outside chasing lightening bugs. I wasn't. I was eavesdropping. Pressing my ear hard against the bottom of our screen door, I'd caught enough of the conversation to form some vague understanding. Mary Lou's transformation confused Dad. He thought she'd grow up to be like his sister-in-law, Miss Elsie…hard working, ever faithful to her parents, modest, humble. I think it was Mary Lou's curves, tight blouses and flouncy skirts that confused the part of my dad still influenced by his family's stubborn Puritanical streak.

But, on her arrival, she was an immediate hit in our neighborhood if one judged by my brother's friends who gathered outside our back door every day.

"Hi boys!" Mary Lou greeted them as if expecting homage.

Besides possessing the natural adolescent male tendencies to put girls off, Bob's friends were both drawn and repelled by Mary Lou. Perhaps they'd overheard their parents discussing how our cousin was just a bit too forward despite coming from a "good family." Perhaps because they felt justified by their own egotism or perceived superiority as males, we began to hear the unfortunate but popular phrase, "Shake it, don't break it." This less-than-friendly echo followed teasings and flirtations which she seemed to take in stride as if all were active shrines to her beauty. I grew tired, however, of hearing the epithet. I even suggested to Mary Lou that perhaps she should only "shake it" in front of the boys, not in front of Mom and Dad lest we move perilously toward the edge of the earth. But Mary Lou never paid attention to social proprieties. She did what she wanted to do. She shook it.

"So what if they get mad?" she asked swinging her head toward me with a straight-line smile and flaring nostrils. "Their lives are so boring. Just like my mom and dad's."

"But…"

"But nothing. It'll give 'em something to talk about." That's what I'm afraid of, I thought as she placed my hand mirror face down on the vanity after checking her ribbon.

"They'll tell your mom and dad for sure," I insisted as if that were a compelling reason to stay on the straight and narrow.

"For goo'ness sakes. Don't you see what's happening? The men's got womenfolk all controlled and everything and no one's havin' any fun!"

I didn't argue because I wasn't sure what that meant. All I knew was that things seemed okay to me. Really okay.

Back then there were so many young people my and my brother's age that just by walking out our front door, we found company…sometimes parties. Kids everywhere. We ran in and out of our friends' homes with no thought of knocking. Doors were never locked because there were no such things as intruders. Even beyond our little neighborhood, there was a freedom to go just about anywhere without adult supervision. There was practically nothing to be afraid of. Our only boogie men were fabricated: the Werewolf, a slow-moving Mummy, Count Dracula, Frankenstein, and Communism.

We were part of the post World War II burgeoning middle class and it felt right…to most of us anyway. Luckily, I was a kid and recipient of the positive side of this new economic order…brand new clothes for school every year, two movies a month with enough money left over for a box of Cracker Jacks; Coca Cola once a week on Saturday nights to go with our spicy chili; three to four really good TV westerns during week nights; cereal box toys like miniature submarines that floated in your sink if you put baking soda in their bellies; and whistles.

17

Fish fries and ice cream socials organized by stay-at-home moms kept our small town vibrant and close. Church services on Sunday mornings were a ritual. Sometimes we gathered at our small white-steepled church on the hill three to maybe even four times a week where we sang, cried and laughed together. And there never seemed to be enough room for all the people in our small sanctuary. Pastors didn't ask for bigger churches in those days, just more chairs.

But even more chairs were inadequate when country singer Buggy Mavens came to visit her old church. The parking lot couldn't hold all the people who came to hear Buggy's nasal top-of-the-chart hits. Those were heady Sundays what with her glittery Nashville entourage in tow and so many of us who'd never even been to Tennessee. She adored our pastor, Brother Milner, who baptized her as a young girl in our big creek down by the county road. I remember watching her in church on Sunday mornings with great interest, along with everyone else, as we flapped our Bilkum Funeral Home fans to stave off insufferable heat. She'd take in our pastor's every passionate fire and brimstone word with glistening eyes after stepping down herself from the podium, her country rendition of "Just a Little Walk with Thee" having raised the skin on our necks. Sometimes it seemed Nashville cast its glittering lights on our small town so often that we were the epicenter of all the excitement it had to offer. And there was Cincinnati's City of Oz skyline down the road sparkling at night to make it all seem true. These images which I conveyed to Mary Lou were, I suspect, the underlying reason for her visit that summer.

The morning before Mary Lou arrived, the first suspicious event of the summer occurred without much notice. Dad and Gilbert, who happened to be Mayor of our small town, teamed up to pull the town drunk out of Mrs. McCullough's flower garden. This, in itself, wasn't all that alarming. They were used to pulling Dugan out of everything...creeks, puddles, other people's cars, large dog houses.

"It's a pity about your flowers, Mrs. McCullough." Dad sympathized, surveying the damage. "It's good you called us when you did. He'd a laid here all day and we'd a had to replace your prize hydrangeas." He winked at our tall, unassuming Mayor who managed a slouch to show his concern.

Mrs. McCullough looked suspiciously at Dad then at his best friend as if to say they still might need replacing. "Dugan's pretty harmless, really," Dad continued, seeming to mediate with the abruptness of a courtroom judge. Then he laughed his quiet, solid laugh that said, "As long as I'm around everything'll be all right." You couldn't dislike my Dad after hearing it.

"I'm pretty sure it was him lookin' in my window last night, I'm tellin' ya." Mrs. McCullough insisted, ignoring Dad's calm reaction to the situation and skillfully pushing renegade strands of silver back under a well-worn gardening hat. "Laws a mercy! Just standin' there big as you please, movin' his head like he was half-crazy or somethin'! Of all the nerve!"

Walking away with her wide straw brim shaking for the shame of it, Mrs. McCullough got in the last word. Unfortunately, we paid little attention to this unlikely description of our town drunk. Had we reflected that Dugan, in all his years of drunkenness, had never been a peeping Tom, perhaps we might have guessed something else was afoot. But Mom and Dad were pre-occupied. Mary Lou was expected to arrive that very afternoon.

It was two o'clock when Mom sent Janey Mullins and me over to keep Mrs. McCullough company. I was asked specifically to observe her hydrangeas and report on their condition later.

"Sure is good lemonade, Mrs. McCullough," I said, trying to get her mind off the flattened area that formed the shape of a small human.

"That's good, honey. You and Janey go inside and get s'more if you want. Some Fig Newtons in the cookie jar. Help yourself. I've got my work cut out for me."

Janey and I pushed Mrs. McCullough's front porch swing backward and forward with jerky shoves and pushes, our legs willing but minds not in concert. The insistent buzz of bumblebees lulled us deeper into summer's entrancing laziness until the swing stood still and greedy quaffing of cold lemonade numbed our throats. Nothing in our sunny world pressed down on us except for the soft burden of play and the decisions necessary to stave off boredom.

"I Dee Diddily, I Dee Dee!" Janey announced, beating me to the punch. With no cue, she laughed out the much practiced words: "I dee diddily, I dee dee. I see something that you don't see. And the color of it is...?"

We were only two minutes into our favorite front porch game when we saw them in slow procession. A line of bunched-up cars made their way past Mrs. McCullough's wide, roofed porch going slower than the thirty-five miles per hour speed limit.

"Here comes your Dad!" Janey pointed to our Pontiac, a brown plump affair that was at the head. Pretending to be aero-dynamic, its constant spewing of smoke made its identity unmistakable.

Five cars followed bumper-to-bumper behind Dad...Dad who was chatting pleasantly and ignoring the honking and swearing that was being leveled at him from behind. One furious beetle-browed driver leaned out beyond his cozy wing, chaffing explosively under the hot summer sun. "Hey bub! Get the lead out!"

But it was no use. I think Dad wanted the whole neighborhood to see him returning home from the bus station carrying my cousin, the summer's prize. With the slow and sure dignity of a chauffeur, Dad parked his car into the crook of our new rock wall just off the road past our mailbox. The angry motorists sped past shouting and leering, unaware of the enchantments they berated. And then it began.

In a trance, we watched Mary Lou spill out of Dad's coupe in all her crinolines and bows. The sun reflected blue off her shiny red hair. She was absolutely one of the girls on my mother's Pond's Cold Cream jar. An almost forgotten symphony, her Lexington accent meandered through Iris and Tiger Lily like an endless river of dreams. By the time it traveled up to our ears through summer's tangle, her long vowels had abandoned their consonants to the somnolent air.

"This is where you le-ive? Maa, it's beautiful!"

High upon the hill sat our modest white house. For her, I think it was a mansion offered up for her first summer's rest from farm work and a blank canvas upon which she would paint the new Mary Lou. She patted her forehead and upper lip with a white embroidered linen. As I watched her arms maintain their ninety-degree bend, limp wrists lifting when her contralto came up dangerously to make a point, I realized Mary Lou had grown up. Her skin still radiated perfect health. Only now, the roses set in her cheeks were nourished by the young surging heart of a romantic. And there was something else. Mary Lou threw her head about in a kind of mockery of her femininity. Her eyes looked skyward and her mouth pursed, flaunting that old strong will as if in hopes someone would call her on it. Immediately I felt uneasy about this when something almost as extraordinary occurred to me for the first time: Mary Lou was not like us. She was, as my mother pointed out later, "very moonlight and magnolias." Dad explained this poetic description. It meant she was Southern.

From out of nowhere young boys began to appear, first just a few, then groups walking nonchalantly toward my Dad's car. Some seemed to suddenly be interested in its lines.

"Mr. Johnson?" Chad, my brother's best friend, approached. "Someone said you've been looking to sell your car." Dad shook his head then smiled at Mary Lou who wasn't fooled.

I abandoned my glass of ice and Mrs. McCullough's front porch, running toward Mary Lou, a source of light brighter than the sun. My lips were sticky with lemonade, my mind a riot of anticipation. Even in that state I was aware of the pungent smell of wild onions growing by the side of the road as they wafted up in clamoring bursts. It was a reminder that spring was ending. Pushing her aside, buxom summer laughed out loud as she made her entrance.

CHAPTER 2

Jake

Given perfect vision that hindsight allows, I now see things clearly. We were overbearing to our neighbors. It was Mary Lou this and Mary Lou that. We dragged her to every single local event, Dad leading her by the elbow, I pulling her by the hand at church functions. Mom cleverly orchestrated Mary Lou's grand entrance by plopping into her hands an elaborate dish—corn pudding, fried chicken or blueberry muffins. This, of course, insured she'd be noticed at the top by the neighborhood and church organizers of each event. As it turned out, all that showing off worked against us. It struck me as odd that no one, especially the young girls of Jefferson, seemed to be as excited about Mary Lou's visit as we were. Why shouldn't they feel honored to meet our beautiful relative, I wondered at a Friday night ice cream social where I made all the necessary introductions. No sooner had I uttered Mary Lou's name in the peach flavor line, then receiving the civil responsiveness of nods and shaking of hands, most people turned away. I expected flattery, gushing, invitations to homes, promises of future visits to our house. But only my dear friend, Janey, indulged my needs. Janey agreed that Mary Lou was "very pretty". It was a severe disappointment as I thought most of the girls Mary Lou's age would surely try to make up to me having a beautiful cousin in tow. I wondered why they couldn't see the advantages. We couldn't keep the boys away from Mary Lou! But the girls kept their distance, robbing me of great triumph.

Besides possessing a classic beauty that was unnecessary to flaunt, my cousin Mary Lou had so many other unique qualities that I'm sure I've forgotten most of them. But some remain firmly in memory. For instance, as I watched her eyes flutter and lips appearing to whisper to the air, Mary Lou gave a general impression that some vague spiritual seismograph lay deep inside her ambitious soul. Often, when its inner tracking devices were verbalized in ooohs and ummms and ahhhs, it was a sign, I soon learned, that she was picking up neglected miracles of life from what seemed miles away or from the microscopic. "Ooooh, is that trillium I see down there by the creek?" All I could see were small yellow flowers not very much in my consciousness. Now they had a name. Or she'd inquire, "Do you s'pose old Schotzy's got a warm place to sleep?" I never gave a second thought to our neighbor's dog who habitually turned over our garbage can in search of scraps du jour. "Does little Janey get enough to eat? Why she's nothin' but skin and bone!"

Then there was the conversation she had with my mother that I heard coming out of the kitchen while they washed and dried dishes.

"Aunt Martha, maybe you just need to do something Uncle Elliot doesn't know about. Like, say, maybe square dancin'. You know, Mom goes to her square dances every other Saturday night. Dad won't go. But his eyes sure light up when he sees Mom in her crinolins and pretty shoes. Maybe that's what you need to do."

How could that work, I wondered. On Saturday nights my mother washed and pin-curled my hair and read my Sunday School lesson to me. Saturday nights were also when she cooked the big Sunday meal that sometimes our Pastor and his wife were invited to and sometimes my Mom's sisters and their families. It was when she ironed my Sunday dress and sewed things up if they needed repair. And Dad liked to watch TV and be waited on for his Saturday night meal knowing that the next day, he would be a footnote in all the activities. The idea that Mom should go out on Saturday nights was preposterous!

Frankly, I was surprised that someone possessing great beauty like Mary Lou's could be all that interested in anyone or anything that did not enhance her own image in some dramatic way. But Mary Lou astonished us at every turn. It took her just under two days to pick up on another one of our neighborhood's neglected miracles. He was ruggedly handsome, made her heart race, and seemed surprisingly unsuited for Mary Lou. That's what my parents said anyway. In all fairness, it was their duty not to encourage her interest in Jake--and for many reasons. It was understood without question back then. He was not boyfriend material.

But it was no use. It was as if she emerged from some unknown planet that gave her a certain freedom of speech not yet witnessed in our go-to-church-three-days-a-week world. In our three-year absence from her, Mary Lou had become what Aunt Bess called a "femme fatale." But, according to Aunt Bess, there was something altogether wrong with the way she used her skills of charm.

"She's goin' to be the ruination of her mother...I can see that a'comin'." Aunt Bess was always positively sure of her predictions and nodded while she spoke, affirming the truth of her words.

The bottom line was my southern belle cousin blinded us. And as far as I could tell, she blinded everyone who happened to be moseying down her social path. But I don't think she ever quite blinded Jake...Jake who, with time, became the proverbial fly in the ointment.

It was one of those first sparkling, early summer mornings that reminds the winter-weary that there can be a heaven on earth after all. I was busy dressing for our first day's shopping adventure. From the corner of my eye, I observed Mary Lou as she powdered her face and sprayed Aqua Net on her thick wavy hair. The upward sweeping design of it mystified me. I was memorizing her every movement when suddenly, like the sound of static electricity before lightening strikes, small rocks pummeled my bedroom screen window. There was a plop at my feet. The plop was Mary Lou. She'd fallen to the floor as if hiding her nakedness. I must have stood there gaping until her little game came clear to me. She was playfully assuming some admirer from below was signaling her. It only could have been one of Bob's friends, I figured, so why all the fuss?

"Get down," she whispered as I stood transfixed at this sudden drama.

She crawled to my dresser where some of her things lay like a pirate's treasure. From this pile of accessories, white dress gloves, beads and pearl earrings, she pulled a pink and white polka-dot scarf. She looked at it thoughtfully, then crawled over to the window, lifted the screen with some difficulty, and held the scarf out the window for just a second. Then she dropped it.

Mary Lou giggled with delight, tensing a vertical finger to her mouth as if I understood she was being very clever. As she sat in a balloon of crepe and crinolines that had puffed up around her legs, I remember the look of bright expectations. She simply glowed as if the first of many fantasies whirling around inside her charmed head had been completed. When sounds of heavy footfalls diminished quickly down the slope of our side yard, we ran to the window to catch a glimpse. But it was too late. I could see it didn't matter. Mary Lou seemed content her scarf was in good hands. I, on the other hand, thought we should run after the thief who stole it. And I would have said so in a burst of anger implicating one of my brother's friends. But suddenly, like seeing for the first time the rolling tide of the ocean, I was struck by an image it's not likely I'll ever forget. With rapturous breathing and smiling broadly, Mary Lou looked out into the canopy of fat-leafed oaks and maples that were level with my second story window. You would have thought their trembling green hands were heaven's door opening for her.

"We'll be right down, Aunty!" Mary Lou yelled breathlessly after being summoned from the bottom of the stairs by Mom's sing-songed "breakfast!" Quickly, Mary Lou found her pop-bead bracelet. *Pop.* It was on. For the life of me, I couldn't figure out how she'd managed with just one hand.

Making a mental note to request pop-beads for my next birthday, I took one last look at myself in the vanity mirror which was something I tried to avoid in those days. It depressed me. My eleven year-old image grated on me more than usual. It was an awkward image. My hair looked lopsided. To make matters worse, there in the mirror next to me smiled Mary Lou, contrasting what I didn't like to think about. My childhood face had vanished, it seemed, over the past two years. Now my face was long and no longer cute. My dimples were still there but no one seemed to notice any more.

"So tell me about your beaux." She was in my face now as if this question burned in her mind.

"I don't even have one beau." I admitted looking quickly away from the mirror with the kind of embarrassment adults wisely ignored in those days.

"Well, do you think I'll find a gorgeous guy while I'm here?" She asked, admiring herself in the mirror.

"Gosh! Why not? I mean…"

"Are there any cute boys in Cincinnati?" She cut me off while hurriedly applying bright orange lipstick to a practiced set of taut lips. "I'm looking for someone who's…you know…divine," she continued looking up at my ceiling that I now realized, too late, was layered in soft, gray cobwebs. Divine? I was confused. It was my understanding, having been brought up in the Baptist church, there had been only one divine man on earth. No doubt reading my thoughts, she continued. "You know, like Tab Hunter."

My stomach churned because I knew Mary Lou expected me to make good on my promise to take her to Cincinnati. Unfortunately, Mom had thwarted those ambitions. She must have suspected some plan like this was hatching because she made it clear the night before Mary Lou's arrival that Cincinnati was strictly out of the question. If we went to town shopping, we were allowed only as far as Covington. "And don't you be thinkin' you can take her by yourself across the river, young lady." This was meant to be a forbidding reminder of my and Janey's recent adventure into the big city without the permission of our mothers. Remembering the consequence of our disobedience, I winced. Switches were still used with great skill in those days.

Later, smelling of bacon and eggs and with Mom in the hallway frantically searching for her keys to the Pontiac, we left the kitchen through the back screen door. My eyes ached from the bright sun. Its slanted morning rays cast long shadows upon a deepening emerald lawn. Directly in front of us, just off the patio, mom's fenced-in English garden appeared surreal after the gray dimness inside. Hummingbirds hovered close within the white-fenced block of color, sipping summer's nectar from a crowd of pink Hollyhocks. Dozens of yellow, purple and blue Swallowtail butterflies pumped their wings showing off their intricate black tracings. A clever mockingbird confirmed all was well-- and so it was except for Bob's friends who loitered behind the flower garden. Making a web of constant motion, fidgeting and pushing each other, they feasted their eyes on the prettiest butterfly: Mary Lou. Chad mumbled they were waiting for Bob to come out so they could play baseball.

"He comin' out soon?" Chad asked in an unconvincing monotone.

"No, he's still in bed," I droned back.

"We'll wait," Chad's voice broke as he stared shamelessly at my beautiful cousin. A shameless Mona Lisa, Mary Lou stared back.

Mom dropped us off at the end of the car line just at the edge of town. There was the usual reminder that I should remember to be a lady. Before she edged the Pontiac back out into the street, she posed us in front of a magnolia tree that graced the side yard of St. Matthew's gothic-style rectory. The ancient tree hung heavy with woody-sweet fragrance and white blossoms. After Mom commanded me to stand up straight, she snapped the picture. I remember how satisfied she seemed to have captured the moment with her Brownie camera. It was the only picture we took of Mary Lou during her visit that summer.

"Bye girls. Have a good time!"

We brushed off some lingering ants that remained from a small crumb of a potato chip someone had left on the wooden bench. Mary Lou and I settled on this weather-worn planking just opposite the bus stop sign. On the back support of the bench was displayed in bright red, black and white paint an advertisement for Coca Cola. Looking as if she could be an advertisement herself, Mary Lou's orange enameled fingernail foraged daintily through her change purse. I watched closely as she counted the quarters and dimes needed for the day's bus fare and lunch.

While admiring this exercise and wondering how soon I would be allowed to wear fingernail polish, a rumbling sound in the distance grew louder as it approached, then stopped directly in front of us. A white Cadillac convertible: long, shining, sleek. Its size and design were formidable even for that era. Mimicking the current popular image of a rocket ship, it gave the impression it was rushing through the air standing dead still. Pink fuzzy dice hung from its rearview mirror. Two teenagers, sitting on the trunk with legs hooked onto the back seat, chewed bubble gum energetically and punched at each other. Chad, my brother's best friend, sat casually behind the wheel.

"Chad!" I yelled. "Where'd you get the car?!"

His timing couldn't have been more perfect. This would surely impress my cousin, my sole purpose and intent for the day. But disappointment followed.

Mary Lou chose to crane her neck toward the corner grocery store just a few feet from our wooden bench as if something there were far more intriguing.

"It's my uncle's," Chad yelled above the music that popped static sounds into the air. "I've been helping him set his crops so he let me borrow it...just for the day. But ain't she a beaut? Can you believe it?"

I couldn't. Chad had wrecked his father's DeSoto the year before. With that, his driving privileges had ended. Since then, like all other guys in the neighborhood, he'd been hitch hiking everywhere. I didn't asked him if his parents knew he was driving his uncle's car.

"Thought maybe you two'd like a ride into Cincinnati. We're goin' that way!" Chad dragged a comb through his waxed-up fins waiting for an answer.

"How'd you know we're goin' to Cincinnati?" I asked, put off that he'd guessed our destination.

"Your brother knows all your little secrets, squirt."

"I swear, Chaddy, if you tell Mom, I'll tell her about the pictures you and Bob draw upstairs."

"Hey, don't sweat it! Come on! Get in. The day's a wastin'."

"Uhhhh, well...OK!" It was too perfect. I forgot my anger and charged up from the bench. But Mary Lou pulled on my skirt and I found myself suddenly next to her again.

"Patti Rae, we can't just hop in that car."

"Why not?" I asked. Hadn't she been talking about meeting guys that very morning?

"Because it wouldn't be lady-like. That's why."

"But Chad's a friend and..."

Mary Lou pressed her white-gloved hand to my gaping, disappointed mouth, glanced at me then peered out of the corner of her widening eyes throwing a coy smile to her admirers.

"Of all the nerve," Mary Lou exclaimed with a pout in their direction.

They laughed back at her as if she'd uttered a secret code. Soon it became obvious I hadn't really been paying attention. With the calibrated movements of a ballerina, Mary Lou pulled her skirt all the way up to her knees as she crossed them. While smiling, pouting, rolling her eyes and generally engaging in unfair flirtation, it occurred to me she wanted them to beg her to get into the car. As she giggled and enticed shamelessly, Chad's slender frame unfurled, slithering out of the driver's seat. His pegged jeans stretched tight against his thin, long legs. Click, click, declack, click, click, declack. It was a sound any respectable teenager made in those days when walking. All six shoe taps beat a loose rhythm on the tense air as he ambled over to our bench, cozying up to a suddenly frozen Mary Lou. It was a show put on for his buddies. But Sammy Morton elbowed Bud, our next door neighbor and my brother's best friend. Sammy giggled in an irritating tenor as if Chad were the dumbest guy on the planet. Chad laid his arm around the back of the bench just above Mary Lou's now recoiling shoulders. Hooking a shiny red strand of hair that lay curled on her back, he twined it around his finger. Mary Lou sat speechless.

"What's wrong?" Chad asked Mary Lou, suddenly straightening up.

"She thinks you're disgusting!" Sammy spit out the "s" sounds with unrestrained contempt, assaulting the morning air with his hyena laugh.

Then, from out of nowhere, another voice:

"She said it wouldn't be lady-like to get in the car! So let's go!"

It was a smooth yet firm command. Its tone was authority and it came from the direction of the back seat. It was Jake's. For some reason, I hadn't noticed his head barely visible from a slouched position. Chad didn't budge.

"Get your butt off that bench or maybe you'd like my fist down your throat!"

I took a second look as the strangely violent command wasn't typically Jake's style. Jake was a whisperer.

Chad stood in disgust, waving both hands in the air at Mary Lou, then strutted back to the car. Dramatically, he collapsed behind the steering wheel resuming a casual one-hand grip. His left elbow hung over the side of the door in a fashionably suave manner appearing so expert that I thought he must have driven his uncle's car hundreds of times.

Widening eyes, an acute reacted smile, a straightened posture…Mary Lou's engines were at full throttle. Her sudden expression of complete rapture seemed to be in reaction to a divinity at once revealed by the pulling back of some invisible crimson curtain. I think it was probably the true beginning of her day, that everything else was forgotten. In Mary Lou's eyes, some creature of perfection now sat center stage even though the sun lit up every nook and cranny of Jake's prematurely aged face.

"Who's Jake?" she whispered separating her question from the gum-chewers with a white-gloved hand to my ear.

"A really nice guy."

It was all I dared say at that point as Jake was within hearing distance. But it was true enough.

"Divine," she breathed out into the crisp morning.

There was that word again, stopping me in my tracks. How, I wondered, could Jake be "divine"?

Mary Lou coyly turned her eyes on me as if I'd been instrumental in conjuring him up. But I was busy thinking. The mystery of her utterance sent me into a lazy exercise of logic: Jake never went to church, I reasoned. So how could he be divine? No white robes swathed him in righteousness and no halo hung over his head. In his usual black jeans and shirt, Jake sat firmly on terra firma. Even at my age, I could see the reality. After a few moments of my best analysis, I decided to leave her to her own impressions. I knew she'd find out about Jake soon enough and I didn't want to ruin the moment.

Jake was the oldest offspring of a highly visible and unforgettable person in our neighborhood. In another time, his father might have been the clown in a Shakespearean play. Unfortunately, his audiences were anything but royal, philosophically inclined or sympathetic to his condition. So, to those of us in the neighborhood who knew him best, he was simply known as the "town drunk."

As sons of drunks often are, Jake was quiet, moody and had an acute distaste for alcohol. He perennially sported a black T-shirt and jeans and gave the impression he could hold his own in any kind of struggle, physical or spiritual. He was referred to as a "hood" or "greaser". But no one would dare call him these names to his face. Bob and his friends held him in high regard even though they didn't dress like him or hang out with his "other" friends. If they had problems with their cars, they took them to Jake. If they had trouble getting a date, they conferred with him. If they needed more money during the week than what was allotted to them by their parents, he parceled out cash in a way that implied he was swimming in it. But lots of cash? That was doubtful even though Jake maintained an evening part-time job as a mechanic at a service station.

One day, Mom and I had stopped for gas at the squat building where he worked at the edge of town. Jake was inside, laboring under a '56 Chevy. A tall, thin teenager in monogrammed denim overalls washed our windshield with a torn chamois. While pumping gas from a shiny red Texaco tank, his rubbery legs led him lazily to each tire as he checked their uneven air pressures. But it was Jake who wheeled his greasy dolly out from under the Chevy engine, stood up stiffly and shuffled into the office to get me a lollipop. He pulled it out of a Mason jar his boss kept full of candy on the front desk.

I thought about that every time we passed by his house on our way home. He and his mother, drunken father and five sisters lived in the unpainted wood frame that was bowed on two sides and whose front porch had long ago given way to gravity. They kept their weeds high as if barriers to their secret pain. But he thought about me, got out from under a broken car, and brought me a lollipop even though he was covered from head to toe in grease.

I remember Jake standing there, seeming to understand my delight and Mom's approval. He gave the distinct impression he'd already experienced every dark side of life but was coming back through again for something else. Sometimes I wondered if the black T-shirt and jeans were the only articles of clothing he owned. Maybe a bunch of them hung in his closet which made it seem as if he wore the same outfit all the time. At least, that's what I liked to think. Whatever, he was the sartorial wonder in our neighborhood, what with the cigarette pack tucked rebelliously into his rolled sleeve and his black boots to top off the James Dean ensemble.

Chad hit the accelerator and white metal fins passed in a screech before the smoke hit us. We coughed with our gloved fists to our mouths but Mary Lou had made her point. She wasn't impressed...with Chad anyway.

We watched the white-finned Cadillac make its departure as waves of heat striped its slowly diminishing space-age image. Suddenly, brakes squealed in the distance. Chad had forgotten a stop sign. Someone in the car whooped and it echoed back to our ears like a summer carnival. It was a wild sound, a loud syllable as expressive of simple joy as anything I've ever heard. Its trailing echo danced in the air like promises of happiness. So we watched intently. The now small white speck lurched right onto Wallace Avenue. Just before disappearing, it looked as if Jake waved. I could have been wrong. But I waved just in case. So did Mary Lou.

—— ◆ ——

Creaking its way through Covington, following the path of ghostly trolley wires from a different era, the city bus carried us through the main shopping districts. I couldn't talk fast enough to keep up with points of interest. They would be helpful to us later when questioned by Mom. Woolworth's Five & Dime, Penney's Department store, Sears & Roebuck. Noticing Mary Lou was consumed by her own thoughts, I continued more earnestly.

"And there's Coppin's Department store where sales ladies put your money in cans that are sucked up into the ceiling. Then pretty soon they come crashin' down a minute later with the right change inside."

Mary Lou nodded, smiling broadly, revealing a perfect row of white teeth.

"Tell Mom we shopped there and your favorite part was the perfume smells and the cans. That'll convince her we were there."

I was in heaven being a sort of off-the-cuff tour guide. I smoothed my white gloves and folded my hands in my lap just like Mary Lou. And the sensation of my eyelashes that Mary Lou had brushed with mascara that morning--they felt heavy and luxurious and I fluttered them like Mary Lou did when she tried hard to get something she wanted. I was just beginning to understand the part mascara played in society.

"We're in Cincinnati!" I announced after our bus squeezed through the narrow openings that led into Dixie Terminal. As we paraded off the bus into the huge cavern of smoke and flitting pigeons along with some twenty other people, I thought I saw Jake exit the front door of the bus.

But I knew that couldn't be possible even though the casual saunter was undeniably Jake's.

"Isn't that the guy who sat in the back seat up ahead?" Mary Lou asked, pointing a gloved finger as we rushed through the wide tunnel that led us into the main part of the building. His face turned our way quickly, and I saw it was Jake after all.

"They must have dropped him off," I said.

"Why would they do a thing like that?"

I could see Mary Lou was concerned that Jake had been thrown out of the car by an angry Chad. So I told her he probably wanted to come by bus since we did. Probably, I assured her, so he could bump into her. She smiled and believed me. The truth was Jake wasn't a group kind of guy. I'd seen him before in the company of Bob's friends. One minute he was the toast of the party, the next he was gone.

As we tramped up the wide marble stairs, grabbing and pulling on a marble and brass banister, Jake disappeared up ahead. Mary Lou craned her neck to keep track of him, but people were moving in all directions and cigar smoke curled up to the ceiling creating a thick haze. And there were the heels of feet in front of us. Special care had to be taken not to scrape them with the toes of our shoes. It was a slow climb with crowds of people to our front and back.

It felt like torture. I was bursting for Mary Lou to see Fourth Street. I imagined the look on her face when finally she would walk down this avenue of high-end retail shops with their colorful windows and impressive designs.

Finally, our pace accelerated, some unseen source pushing Mary Lou and me out of the high-ceilinged halls of Dixie Terminal. The hordes swerved around us quickly disappearing into the arteries of a throbbing, vibrant city. Only Mary Lou and I stood still. This unconscious act, alone, caught the attention of a small man standing alert by the side of the terminal.

CHAPTER 3

Beguiled and Begotten

"Excuse me, Ma'am."

"Huh?" I said. Mary Lou and I turned to see if the small man standing close to the Dixie Terminal building had actually addressed us.

"Is it not a beautiful day?"

He spoke like a politician and there seemed no doubt he directed his remarks our way. His snagged, once handsome suit showed lint unsuccessfully brushed. He stood rigid in aristocratic posture but there was the greasy hair. It was combed carefully, but I remember there seemed to be some question of cleanliness.

"Yes," Mary Lou's sudden smile surprised me. She bent her pretty head down toward the intruder who sidled up to her like a tame cat.

"I hope you don't mind me saying that I've not seen beauty such as yours in a very long time!"

It wasn't Mary Lou's eyes that betrayed the effect of this compliment. It was her hand on my arm that said "don't miss this". Her compliant stance…head lilting to one side, hands now folded upon the other…begged for more. Her broad smile fell softly upon this swarthy complexioned man, innocently taking away any protective barrier against his motives we might have had otherwise. I grabbed her arm to pull her away. But their eyes locked.

"Shopping in the big city today, are we?"

"Yes!" Mary Lou was quick to respond but then looked back to make sure he was talking to her and not someone else. "And this is my cousin who's showin' me around. This is my first day here in Cincinnati." Giggling, she was obviously pleased to have the admiration of an older man.

"So you are your cousin's sole escort today?" the tame cat continued with a look of fawning admiration that was supposed to make me believe I was as pretty as Mary Lou. Maybe just as important. My eyelashes, I thought. So I batted them like Mary Lou.

"Yes sir," I said. "I know my way around pretty good. I come shoppin' over here lots of times with my mom, so we don't need any help. But thanks a lot."

Another giggle burbled up from Mary Lou like a geyser. He puffed out a short laugh.

"I can see you're in expert hands." Speaking directly to Mary Lou now, he glanced around as if expecting someone as he folded and re-folded a newspaper previously wedged under his arm.

"Still in high school, young lady?"

Mary Lou lied, saying she was a Freshman in college, so sure she was of her fully matured body. Gesturing hands, timed dramatically with his sometimes halting speech, the stranger seemed to feel his security now in the conversation. Mary Lou watched them in a trance.

"Where are you from, if I may be so bold?"

"La-ex-ing-ten," Mary Lou cooed in the softest lilt ever to come out of Kentucky.

"Lexington," he repeated slowly as if he wanted to digest what that meant or recollect something or someone from that area. "I'll bet you were Miss Lexington at one time."

Mary Lou shook her head, the gold of the sun glinting off her orange halo.

"Well, at least you must have been the prom queen?"

She shook her wavy red hair again, still smiling and maybe encouraging this man more than she should, I thought.

"No?"

"No sir," she drawled. "There're lots of pretty girls in Lexington. Lots more prettier than me."

What greater beauty could outshine hers, I wondered. Eyeing her carefully, trying to bring objectivity made available by my few years of experience,

I concluded she was lying. So I gave her credit for being humble. Then he said, "I find that hard to believe."

"Honest." She insisted. It gave him time to throw more compliments her way.

"If I were the Mayor of Lexington, this Mayor would crown you Queen and there's no doubt about that."

"Really?" she piped as if it mattered what he thought.

It was then that it welled up inside of me. Fear. Struggling to breathe, I tried to control its expansion in my chest. I remember my thoughts racing: Why was I feeling this way? Perhaps it had to do with Mom's aversion to conversations with strange men. I remembered how she'd grabbed me in an elevator once when a stocky man in blue jeans mentioned I'd be a beautiful woman some day. It frightened Mom somehow that I'd smiled at him.

But this man was different, unique. He seemed to pose no danger. He was nice, actually. Still, fear stared me down and I felt I had no other choice. So I slipped directly behind Mary Lou and, with a short crisp tug at her skirt invisible to his fawning eyes, I signaled, thinking she might make an exit. But she never wavered and took in his next remark as if the world had suddenly been laid at her feet.

"Well, looks like I'm going to have to visit Lexington again real soon. I scout around for models down there, you know. That's my job."

Mary Lou almost gulped. Her next words were chosen carefully.

"Last year I was Miss Autumn in the Fall Horse Festival parade. Did you see me riding on the float?" She asked conferring on him a ubiquity that seemed to both embarrass and please him. He had to admit he hadn't. But he looked cleverly disappointed as if not seeing her on the float was his greatest loss.

"I fear I did not," his head dropped slightly.

"They took me right through downtown. I was wavin' and wearin' an autumn leaf crown that my mom made from real maple leaves!"

He watched her smile intently.

"Are you sure you didn't see me?"

It didn't matter. His mission was accomplished. Even though it appeared she was in control, I began to understand it was a clever function of his allowed illusion. He had her in his grip, and I watched amazed at the way she inclined her body toward him, how she waved her pretty gloved hands in his direction and turned as if smiling at a ghost, allowing him to view the fullness of her silhouette more closely.

"May I introduce myself," the princely-acting man continued seeing his chance. "My name is Herbert Von Stroben and I am owner of Von Stroben Modeling Agency in the Carew Tower."

He was obviously proud of this fact. He stood ramrod straight with his head tilted quite high into Mary Lou's face.

"A modeling agency?" Mary Lou squealed.

"Yes ma'am. I take it that, with your unprecedented beauty, surely you have considered modeling at one time or another."

Mary Lou stammered. "Well, I don't know that I…well, a teacher once told me that I had the…"

"I know this sounds a bit rushed," he interrupted, "but I'd like to interview you and show you around to my staff and perhaps do a bit of photographing. Of course, only if you have the time that is." Then he looked at me as if I might object. My fear had receded into a manhole and suddenly I embraced the magic. I nodded my head quickly with brows lifted indicating the decision was Mary Lou's.

"I would like to capture the essence of your porcelain-like skin," he continued becoming more confident with each minute.

Mary Lou was enraptured.

"See that dress across the street?" He asked pointing elegantly to a lime-green frock in one of Percy-Rembrandt's windows. It was the most expensive shop in town. Only a week before, I had overheard my mother telling her friend that Mrs. Barstow, our town's much-revered piano tutor, purchased a fifty-dollar suit there and that didn't include the shoes and bag she bought to go with it. By the time she left the boutique, her expenses totaled $100!

Mary Lou turned around demurely. She squinted and searched out the dress despite the crowds that passed in front of it. She nodded.

"Wouldn't you look lovely in that dress?" He asked with his eyes pinned on her from out of their corners. I thought of the biblical serpent in the Garden of Eden.

Mary Lou's smile said it all. She agreed. He then produced a slightly soiled card, waving his name and some other information printed on it in front of her face. She reached out to pluck the card but he yanked it away excusing himself for not giving it to her. It was his last card. He needed to have more printed. But would she allow him to purchase the aforementioned dress as a gift to her for her first photographic session? Compliments of the agency, of course.

"Why," Mary Lou said breathing in. "I couldn't let you do that. I…" she said breathing out, convincing me she meant it.

"Nonsense." He said. "Size eight?" He guessed.

She nodded hesitantly.

And would she wait for him just outside the door until he had the dress in hand?

As we stood outside Percy-Rembrandt's stately marble entrance making way for shoppers entering the heavy brass doors, Mary Lou repeated the words roiling through my own mind: "I can't believe it! I can't believe this is happenin'!" I shook my head a bit nervously simply because I couldn't either. But she smiled in ecstasy as if all were as it should be. I had heard from my older city cousins that Cincinnati was brimming over with modeling agencies. Somehow this thought calmed me. And considering the fact that Mary Lou seemed to have hit upon something she really wanted to do, suddenly I was glad we'd met this strange man.

Eventually we became aware of a knot of women shoppers huddled just inside one of the windows nearby. Just beyond them stood elegantly dressed and colorfully made-up women behind white, enticing counters. One by one, these painted ladies offered up vials of fragrances to customers' sniffing noses. I shadowed Mary Lou through the door with caution, her wide eyes searching all the while for Von Stroben. He was nowhere in sight. We shot over to the popular perfume counters. Almost immediately, Mary Lou allowed a sales woman--Anna was her name according to her nametag--to spray something lavish on her. It smelled just like Mrs. McCullough's pink roses.

"Joy," she explained to Mary Lou, "is the most expensive perfume in the world."

I waited for Mary Lou to ask her how much but she never did. She inquired about another fragrance that was contained in a larger, more ornate bottle with a hat-like top. "Josephine" was written across the front of the expensive-looking flask. Mary Lou took in its fragrance with Anna becoming quite excited, although I didn't know why. The look dissipated, however, when Mary Lou excused herself explaining we were needed outside. But, in an instant, Anna brought out another handsome vial of perfume.

While she and Mary Lou discussed which fragrance would best suit her, two dark male forms appeared at a nearby window. With hands cupped around their eyes, I could see their glances were in our direction. One wore what looked like a helmet but it was difficult to tell who they were and what they were doing as they stood in the shadow of Percy-Rembrandt's awning. I imagined they were looking at Mary Lou.

Beyond these two silhouettes, the sun cast its brilliant light on the other side of the street. There, casually slumped and seeming ever the James Dean, I saw Jake once again in the company of Chad, Sammy and Bud. A cigarette dangled loosely from his mouth as he leaned against a building, hands resting in his pockets, while his overly excited friends discussed something not interesting to him. Hanging like an afterthought between Jake's arm and waist was a bouquet of roses wrapped carefully in tissue paper. It was a brilliant foil against his black t-shirt and tight pants. He flung his shortened cigarette to the ground, stepped on it, then lifted the yellow petals to his nostrils taking in the fragrance in much the same way Mary Lou inhaled the costly perfumes. Unlike Mary Lou, however, Jake's eyes seemed fixed on some vision of inner peace, some understanding of the universe that I imagined was now changing in landscape and atmosphere by an encroaching image of Mary Lou.

Meanwhile, Mary Lou dabbled in a luxury of smells beyond the dimes and quarters in her change purse. Her eyes were wild with adventure suggesting needs I didn't understand and an impatience to satisfy them. It wasn't long after that Von Stroben reappeared with a Percy-Rembrandt's bag in hand.

He seemed angered to find us inside. He motioned for us to exit through the main door with noticeable impatience.

"Follow me girls," he whispered coarsely. I tried to direct Mary Lou's attention to Jake with his bouquet of roses I suspected might be for her. But she was pre-occupied with the unique bustle of city life, the parade of mid-western culture and the dull flat sounds of speech falling on her southern ears.

As we rounded the corner of Fourth & Vine, some greasy-looking characters, appearing bored, suddenly grew inspired. They obviously recognized our escort for the important person he was. Standing at military attention, they greeted him as Herr Von Stroben. One man even called him "the Captain" and brought himself up in a perfect salute. Our pace had been quick but upon approaching these vagrants, Von Stroben slowed down. My pace had not slowed, however, and I found myself next to Von Stroben. Looking up at his finely chiseled profile, I caught a momentary glimpse of exaltation. It seemed to materialize from this chance meeting of derelicts who, by their salutations, had conferred a feeling of importance upon him. I thought their admiration gave him a glory beyond their powers to impart. Still, his own self-importance radiated up into the atmosphere so clearly that the contagion of it fell upon me like sparkling confetti. Suddenly, I felt important too.

Just seconds after, his gait quickened again and Mary Lou and I found ourselves running in order to keep up with the Captain. Crossing the street before the cross walk, we were able to enter Pogue's Arcade more quickly. This formidable arched hallway tunneled under the highest skyscraper in Cincinnati, the Carew Tower. The arcade was all bustle and motion like the street outside. Stainless steel fans supported by tall pedestals stood like sentinels along the way, forcing warm air on overheated shoppers. Bristol's Jewelry store with its sparkling diamonds enticed Mary Lou to its window. But I watched Von Stroben carefully as he slithered through the crowd, so we were able to run and catch up with him. Through the soft billowing of memories, I can still hear "Moon River" playing from somewhere. As we walked on, Elvis' "Ain't Nothin' But a Hound Dog" replaced the more soothing melody. We passed three banks of elevators then followed our modeling guru into a stairwell that was dimly lit.

"We'll take the stairs, girls," he announced turning quickly. I remembered thinking how it seemed he thought we might have disappeared. "The elevator takes too long and I'm only on the second floor."

Sounded reasonable to me. But as we traipsed up the first set of stairs, lingering in the air was a strong smell of urine that turned my stomach. I wished we'd taken the elevators.

"Now," the man stopped and turned again looking at Mary Lou as we stood on the first landing. "What did you say your name is?"

"Mary Lou."

"Now Mary Lou, before I introduce you to my staff...and I probably failed to tell you how picky they are in their tastes...I feel it's my duty to first take a professional look at your legs."

I looked at Mary Lou's legs and wondered what his imagination, which surely he must have as a modeling agent, could not tell about them. Any fool could see they were long and shapely despite her full skirt. Was he blind?

Thinking that he still might have sun spots in his eyes, I began a description of her great tree-climbing abilities that I'd witnessed a few years back when we'd visited my uncle's farm. Then, suddenly, with a practiced flourish, Herr Von Stroben lifted her skirt and crinolins over her head, baring her legs, garter belt and panties. For a split second I perceived I was witnessing a professional at work despite the shame of her exposure to the dank, concrete stairwell. A motion so natural, it seemed to me, must come from professional practice. But then Mary Lou's scream pierced the vertical corridor and my naïve bubble burst like a thousand firecrackers.

Before I could gather my wits, the door to the landing opened in a dizzying flash. Two policemen rushed toward us. One of the burley figures wore a helmet...the helmet I'd seen through Percy-Rembrandt's window. They grabbed Von Stroben in some vague, fomenting anger.

"Okay," the shorter of the two shouted with snarling lips. "Having some more fun, are we? That's the last time you'll be doing this."

He handcuffed the indignant Herr Von Stroben right in front of us. With a yank, he whisked him out into the hallway where the policeman and his

41

partner had been waiting in ambush. We heard Von Stroben shouting expletives through the closed door. Somehow it didn't sound like him.

The other rather tall policeman cast a long shadow over us, eyeing our quivering forms as if we should be ashamed of ourselves. Taking our names and scribbling quickly on a small pad, he asked if we were hurt in any way. But all we could talk about was the modeling agency and the unnecessary embarrassment Mr. Von Stroben had caused. Had the gentleman lost his mind? What would the people at the modeling agency think of him when they heard about this? Then we noticed the Percy-Rembrandt's bag. Mary Lou grabbed it with both hands expecting the heaviness of a dress. But it was light as air. Just tissue paper inside and a bit of ribbon.

"Ladies," the policeman continued booming his impatient baritone. "Where are you from?"

"La-ex-ing-ten," Mary Lou cooed for the second time that day as if someone had flipped a switch. Looking in the bag had turned her bewildered look into a frown, then confused embarrassment. But that lasted as long as it took her to realize destiny had once again provided another man from which to coax admiration.

But I continued stammering, still in shock while Mary Lou and the policeman fell into a soft conversation considering how it began. Mary Lou's white-gloved hand pulled me down the stairs as she prattled on. I listened, trying to decide what was really happening, when somewhere between the second and first floor, there came to me in the suffocating air, my first real adult crisis. Thoughts of eternal damnation for what I had gotten Mary Lou into fell upon me with unrelenting weight. Mary Lou had been shamed and it was all because of me. The logic was simple. It was my fault because I'd brought her to Cincinnati against my mother's wishes! I wanted to run home and tell Mom what I had done so she could comfort me. But I had lied to her. I had told her we would only go as far as Covington. This time, finding solace in my mother's arms wasn't an option.

A heavy guilt left me in a nauseous state, not just because I had lied but also because we had been taken advantage of as women. I could hear our pastor on Sunday morning at the podium. "Favor is deceitful, and beauty is vain, but a woman who feareth the Lord, she shall be praised." But was there a scripture for women who had been hoodwinked? Would we get a break for being led like sheep? It was too frightening to imagine how this one small incident could come crashing down on my mother's world, destroying it and the image of her daughter, not to mention her niece. But even more frightening, I imagined how we must look in God's eyes. As I bravely fought back the tears, the smell in the stairwell plunged me into a deeper, emptier despair I had only once experienced at the age of four before taking anesthetic for a tonsillectomy. On top of that, I was confused. Mary Lou was giggling, talking in a playful manner and, as difficult as it was for me to imagine, having fun.

Once out of the dismal stairwell, the tall policeman led us back into the street where his motorcycle awaited him curbside. I hadn't noticed his high black boots and handsome face until he straddled his wide, shiny chromed bike. Grabbing his helmet from under his arm and with a studied nonchalance, he covered his dark curls then strapped leather beneath his chin. I could see it in Mary Lou's eyes. Divine.

"Ladies," he said with a grin and with a lighter tone than earlier. "Now stay out of trouble and don't go trailing after bums any more today. I've got enough to worry about."

Bums? What was he talking about? But Mary Lou giggled with a knowing look. She smiled and waved goodbye as he called back in a mockery of Mary Lou's accent. "Ya'll be careful now, ya hee-a?" It was mean of him, I thought. Even worse, it was a terrible impersonation.

Mary Lou said she would, and I waved feverishly before he even left the curb, so eager was I to be rid of him. Then his bike sputtered its poison into the already stale air as he pulled away. A knot of pedestrians waiting for a green light stared as if we were marked as criminals. So Mary Lou yelled after the divine creature, ignoring his unkind mockery and making it clear to everyone we'd only been helped out of a difficulty. "Why, it's awful nice of you to help! Thanks ever so much!"

If she had not taken the insult, I had. I wanted to put my hand to her mouth. But Mary Lou gave me a wink, as if he were just another incident along life's way. Then she shook it but didn't break it, maneuvering her way back through the turnstile door and into the arcade with me following in a slump.

Before entering, I cast dark and gloomy eyes back out into the noisy street and saw the vibrant colors of the passers-by—the feathers in ladies' hats waving stiffly in the breeze, their shopping bags and hat boxes of all colors and designs, the deep hunter green of a window canvas flapping casually in summer's yawn, a hot-dog vendor engrossed in brisk business under his bright red umbrella. So much beauty and life as usual passing behind me despite what had happened. And, on top of that, utterly incomprehensible to me, the sun was still shining.

If I had not caught sight of Jake standing quietly by the door as we re-entered the arcade, I believe the memory of each detail of that very minute may have been lost in a month, maybe a year. But they live on in my mind to play over and over again; childhood images unshorn of their mysteries.

CHAPTER 4

Hungry Like a Wolf

Like a pack of wolves, they huddled abruptly, determining their chances as inexperienced predators. Their eyes shifted from Mary Lou to each other. A group of seven teenage boys out on the town, unchaperoned. As they passed, bumping against each other, I held my breath. But they did pass. Though aggressive looks were cast our way, there was doubt as they looked back, still determining. Before exiting the door, one left a cat call echoing high off the curved ceiling. Hot waves of heat beamed from my face as other heads, then bodies, then a complete domino effect of attention gravitated our way. All were looking at them. Mary Lou's twisting hips in full semi-circle motion. Slowly, evocatively to the left, then to the right...left, right.

My first impulse was to disappear into a corner. And I wanted to drag Mary Lou with me. I imagined that maybe I could plead with her. But if I did this —even though it was unlikely I would— what, I asked myself, would I tell her? Mulling this over anxiously as if some huge moral construct would cave in without my intervention, I continued to watch and followed like a lemming. Laboriously working her hips in Marilyn Monroe style and scouting for those who would surely be watching, I think Mary Lou expected some ruggedly handsome man to whisk her away. I realize now she must have watched the same movies that I watched and was familiar with the same movie stars. They had slipped irreversibly into my consciousness back then despite my Dad's insistence that modern entertainment was evil. Marilyn Monroe with her hips and whispering innuendo, Doris Day with her defiant independence. They were the more obvious ones. There were

45

also the black and white classics shown on Saturday mornings. Marlene Deitrich, Ava Gardner and other sirens who brought sensuality into the living rooms of unwitting Americans. These femme fatales were never without a red-blooded male in flagrantly hot pursuit.

An occasional man, in passing, did spin around to watch my cousin. And some women shook their heads for the shame of it. I saw a little girl mimic the pretty lady in green, screech-laughing. Her mother's eyes widened in shock. But where was that male in hot pursuit?

Mary Lou's antennae searched the corridor for him. But no Cary Grant appeared. No David Niven strode by her side, hand on elbow, ready to navigate her into ecstasies yet unknown.

"Come on! Dontcha wanna see what's in here?" Mary Lou asked calling back to my slumped figure. I suspected she secretly giggled at my embarrassment.

By conveniently ignoring me, she hadn't seen Jake following us, I realized. But I had. In a fraction of a second I'd caught his reflected image through a door swung slowly open just before I passed it. The three of us, I pretending not to see Jake, walked on in a sort of casual parade. She at the head, I in the middle, Jake the caboose. We passed windows displaying temptations offered up by Pogue's Department Store. First, there was the Hat & Glove Department, then the Wine Cellar, Meats, Notions, Handbags until we made our way to the west end of the arcade. At this more glamorous spot where retail enticements gave way to opulent interior, Mary Lou stopped suddenly with arms out and palms up. It was her way of communicating an unexpected treasure.

There in mysteriously lit temptation, a broad winding marble and bronze stairwell led up from the Arcade into that deluxe structure known as the Netherland Plaza Hotel. I was immediately struck by its perfect setting for a Ginger Rogers & Fred Astaire dance. I could imagine them in all this opulence, their shoes tapping ingenious rhythms upward. The mellow lights casting gold upon shining brass was surely a beckoning to the brightest, the richest, the most handsome to ascend to this high order. Once there, my mind's eye followed these sleek paradigms of city life as they disappeared into private corners where fashionable lunches and rendezvous played out in their dark palm-hidden spaces. Just like in the movies. From the look on her face, I felt sure Mary Lou was pretty much imagining the same things.

"Are you okay?" Jake plied casually in her ear. He had drifted by me placing a strong hand on my left shoulder as if to navigate better toward Mary Lou. Then he approached her back that was turned in complete absorption of this new heaven's gate. Anyone else would have jumped, I thought. She only just turned toward Jake with a delighted but distracted look. It was maybe two seconds before she responded. Then slowly, through a maze of colliding realities, it came to her that the casual interrupter was Jake. Jake, knight in shining armor, had materialized at a most inopportune moment. I think now, looking back, she didn't need him nor did she need anyone at this juncture of allure and adventure.

"I'm fine. Really." She fluttered her eyelashes and I worried how she would explain the policeman or if she even realized he might be referring to our recent run-in with the Captain.

"Are those roses for me?" She asked looking down at the full bouquet wrapped in pink tissue that appeared newly worn at the edges. The diversion, if it was one, was clever.

"Do you like yellow roses?" Jake asked.

"Yes," she said breathing in their fragrance, her mouth forming into something like a pouting smile, a promised kiss.

"Well then. It's settled. They're for you."

With some rattling of tissue paper and an "ooohing" from her inner engines, Mary Lou gathered up the roses Miss America style. Conveniently an ornate, full-length mirror just to the left of the stairwell offered itself up for self-adulation. Finely tuned to her own sense of self, it seemed Mary Lou's instincts told her one must pose before one can become immortal. So she stood in a sort of stage posture for one or two seconds smiling broadly at her image. Jake smiled back at her through the looking glass. It was an awkward smile.

"I like you, Jake," she announced to the mirror, as if she needed a verbal prompting to snap out of her self-absorption.

But Jake turned to her in an effort, it seemed, to force Mary Lou to address him directly. She continued to view his dark clothes in a way that appeared unrelated to reality like Alice through the looking glass, interpreting that up is down and right is left.

"I like you..." He began awkwardly avoiding her Wonderland eyes, "...especially with my flowers."

The words crashed down on her like broken crystal.

"I thought they were my flowers." Mary Lou's dreamy gaze disappeared.

"Of course, they're your flowers but before that, they were mine."

Mary Lou bristled.

"You did buy them for me, didn't you?"

During this temporary wreckage of Mary Lou's ego, she turned from the mirror and considered Jake's image differently now.

"Actually, I bought them for myself," Jake said straightening his shoulders. "And I thought, if I'm lucky, I'll meet someone sweet and pretty to give them to."

"Oh," Mary Lou purred in recovery. "Aren't you the dearest?"

The balance came tentatively and, for just a second, I felt like running. But she had demurred and I saw for what reason she stalled the flow of conversation. The beckoning stairwell. She cast several glances toward it as if a lover waited impatiently for her upstairs. "So, have you ever been up these here stairs?" Mary Lou inquired with her head cocked toward Jake's, her eyes playfully suggesting she wanted nothing more than to try her feet on their smooth marble surface.

But Jake's thoughts and glances flowed in the direction of Mary Lou alone who stood just inches away. He took in her hair and the simple fragrance of Evening in Paris cologne as if viewing and smelling a foreign country for the first time. I saw then that the clouds Jake and Mary Lou floated upon were equal in passion and illusion. Somehow they seemed to see romantic particles hovering in the air, invisible fairy dust to the uninitiated. I wondered what might be going through his mind. Maybe he saw her in his arms and could taste the orange lipstick that shone on her mouth like candy. I half expected him to say anything to impress her...that possibly he knew the hotel well enough that he would follow her up the stairs. That maybe he would spend what money he had left from service station work and pretend that this was his world. But he didn't.

"I thought you came to town to go shopping?"

"Well, a girl can snoop around, can't she?"

Jake didn't answer.

"There's just so much to see. I want to see it all! You know what I mean?"

"Sure!" He said. But I suspected he didn't.

He looked lost. Smoothing nervously the ducktail canal at the back of his head, a sort of mechanized part of a mind at work, he appeared to struggle with some thought.

"Hey. Why dontcha let me buy you a root beer float up there on the ice cream bridge?" He pointed up to the heavens where one section of the mezzanine was filled with white filigree tables and chairs overlooking the arcade. It took Mary Lou just a moment to filter this new enchantment through her storehouse of dreams.

"Okay!" She beamed. "An ice cream bridge?"

The unnecessary question echoed through the arcade each time she repeated it. "An ice cream bridge?" She'd never heard of such a thing.

We followed Jake…I skipping after him, Mary Lou sashaying with his yellow roses fragrant against her breast. I thought I could hear her heart beating a rapid pulse against their soft innocence.

Up ahead, I could see that Jake's usual sleepy shuffle had disappeared as if someone had told him he'd never have to work another day in his life… that from here on out, no dream was too big to serve up to his delicate, wildly beating desires.

I watched Mary Lou's hips follow the lithe, now joyful Jake. As proprietary as a store clerk, he led us away from the Netherland intrigue, out of the arcade and back inside the department store. Ascending the escalator, he appeared intimately familiar with its destination.

Once on the mezzanine bridge, he chose the perfectly placed table and chairs. I remember being amused as I watched him. It was as if this one decision could possibly change his entire life. I plopped down in the chair he indicated and remembered to fluff my crinolines. Then I took in the activity all around me in a sort of dream. Looking down through the mezzanine glass bridge in an effort to see it through Mary Lou's wistful eyes, I was pleasantly surprised.

"One root beer float, please." Mary Lou ordered herself. This didn't seem to please Jake. I think he wanted to do it for her, to be master of her new experience. So his control and restraint seemed admirable when he ordered for me. Never, however, did he take his eyes off Mary Lou...Mary Lou who was missing nothing. Not the white starched waiter's jacket, not his paper hat, not the people passing by carrying silk-roped hat boxes and shopping bags, but especially not the people walking one story below us visible beyond the protective glass where we'd been only minutes before.

In one of those moments of intense impressions, I cast a more sensitive eye downward into the echoing arcade. It was funny. I'd walked through this long rotunda a hundred times in the past. But only now did I consider its qualities and unique beauty. It seemed to me it had all been brought about by some stark mathematician who saw things in terms of cold symmetry with a smattering of ancient Egyptian art. Its allure of incongruity and exotic fantasy seized upon my imagination until I gave in completely to the illusion that we were really somewhere. The center of the universe could have been suggested to me at this point, and I would have wholeheartedly agreed.

"Dad says this arcade's all Art Deco," I said, sure that this bit of information would impress Mary Lou.

"Art Deco," she whispered as her eyes scanned the scene below. It was obviously not a term she understood, which was too bad, because I didn't either.

"All I know," her voice was now monotone, trapped in the moment, "is that it's real pretty. Look at all that shiny stuff all over the walls and where do all those people come from, do you think?"

"I don't know," I sighed, "but they're sure in a sweat to get somewhere."

She nodded as she sipped hard at a few last pieces of solid ice cream after which she laughed for no good reason it seemed.

Then Mary Lou grasped Jake's hanging hand inspired by something I couldn't see. I'd noticed people at church who took up hands like that when wanting someone's undivided attention. She whispered a "thanks" in his ear or at least it seemed it should be something like that. I watched their intense attraction for each other as if viewing a movie in the privacy of my own home. But my prying eyes unnerved Mary Lou. With a quick turn, she asked if I required the use of the restroom. It was close and wouldn't that be a good idea? She didn't have to say more.

By some great fortune, I found a large white supporting pole on my way to what the department store chose to call the "Ladies Powder Room". I slipped behind it quickly and discovered I could continue spying on my cousin and Jake as they brushed up together, both confident their privacy was assured by a busy, anonymous public.

Three feet behind the pole where I stood, sat an older woman with a young girl of about five dressed in white eyelet and lace. The woman's cheeks were heavily rouged in two almost perfect circles. Her eyebrows artificially arched high toward her stiff curled bangs. I think the bangs were supposed to give her an air of youth. This attempted illusion was cancelled out, however, by fire engine red lipstick that traced imaginary full lips over thin ones. Two mountains of red just under her hooked nose. The overall effect made me jump. But I don't think she noticed. The little girl giggled.

"Look, Gramma! That girl's hiding so they don't see her." Rushing out of her ice cream chair, she bounced toward me but grandmother caught her arm.

"Quiet, Darling," grandmother said in an overly sweet command and led a tiny behind back into its chair.

I smiled gratefully at "Gramma" for helping me stay under cover. After a few moments I looked back at them. They were so quiet, grandmother and grandchild. It seemed they had decided that staring at Mary Lou and Jake would be fun too. So there were three of us now spying. They'd forgotten their tuna salad sandwiches cut into triangles, potato chips and Coca Cola. To them as well as everyone else it seemed, as I cast my eyes around at other tables, the image of the pretty girl and the less than appropriate-looking young man could not be resisted.

Suddenly I was a leader of spies. Everyone was leaning in their chairs or scooting to a new position in order to stare better at the sight. Staring in those days was perfectly acceptable public behavior if something presented itself that wasn't by the books.

As I and my fellow spies watched without shame, Jake put his hand on the back of Mary Lou's chair. This she didn't seem to mind. I thought of poor Chad who had tried that very tactic earlier in the day and had been spurned. All Mary Lou noticed at this point, I think, were Jake's large eyes and heavily lashed eyelids that drooped sleepily. They followed Mary Lou's every move. But more interesting, they appeared to be memorizing every detail of Mary Lou's face for a time when, perhaps, she would no longer be around. That seemed not too improbable as I looked on with some shock at their differences. Mary Lou's skin was slightly moist and supple from a diet of fresh country eggs, vegetables, fruits and meat. Jake's was taut and grayish, even though tanned, from a diet that probably seldom saw vegetables or fruits. To make things worse, Jake smoked as she giggled into the still fresh air that he and a few others close by were quickly fogging. His habit would soon etch wrinkles into his face, I thought. I remembered the photos of my Uncle Teddy's once smooth and rosy skin that had recently given in to the poisons of tobacco. But for now, Jake's shocking light blue eyes, like those of gray wolves, shone above cheeks reddened with excitement.

Mary Lou responded with enthusiasm to most of what he said.

"You did? Well I can just see you doin' that!" She showed keen interest in the stream of stories emptied into her ears without restraint. I wondered if these whisperings invited her into the sad side of his life or if they were stories tidied up for her sensitivities that he surely must have guessed at.

"…and that dress you have on…" he was on a roll. "…nothing like that in Percy-Rembrandts…"

Whatever, Jake was now in control. And I thought it gave him an air of confidence that had been lacking in the arcade. I couldn't help but notice, also, that he kept his hands out of view. One was behind her chair. The other dropped down by his side dangling a Camel's cigarette. They were worn hands, torn and bruised by premature hard labor. Fidgeting and grasping, they would have betrayed his nervousness had she seen them. But Jake kept them hidden and spoke softly, taking in the creamy color of Mary Lou's hands now that her white cotton gloves had been peeled away. He must have wondered at their opalescence, not so much a color but a statement of delicacy. They were very likely the most beautiful hands he'd ever seen.

"You didn't!" she said flinging throaty vowels up into cascading giggles.

In Jake, I believe she wanted some masculine dedication to her safety and something else not yet quite obvious. I somehow knew as I watched, that her most pressing need was his finely chiseled face and its close proximity when a kiss imagined would surely come. Intoxicated, she followed the whispers escaping his mouth like pivoting air. How differently I see him, I thought. I considered his battered black boots firmly planted beneath the table. I don't think their dirty surface had ever seen polish or brush.

When I figured enough time had passed, I returned to the table with heavy footfalls so they could hear me. Jake sat back conforming to a respectful distance from Mary Lou. For the next fifteen minutes or so, he paid us equal attention. I looked around hoping that, now, I also was in everyone's focus. But it seemed the curiosity seekers had gone back to their noontime repasts without interest. It was as if they understood. Nothing too shocking could happen with me at the table. With a feeling of disappointment I watched, too late, a hungry Jake finish off my chocolate malt.

"I thought you weren't hungry, Jake," I protested because I hadn't finished.

"I'm not. I just don't like to waste food."

I scoffed at this but then I noticed how thin he was for having such large wrists. His squared shoulders also appeared in need of flesh. If I'd only drunk half my malt, there would have been more left for him, I thought. He may be running out of money, I also reasoned, allowing my pity to overshadow the fun I was supposed to be having.

"Did I tell you Patti Rae's my girlfriend?" Jake asked looking at me, then Mary Lou with a wink of an eye he imagined I couldn't see.

"Oh, Jake! I am not!"

"Yes, you are. Remember, last week I gave you that Cracker Jacks ring?"

"Yeahhh."

"And remember I told you it meant we were goin' steady."

"Yeah, but…" and I looked at Mary Lou.

With the sides of her mouth curling up from a forced frown, she considered me out of the corner of her eyes. It was one of her many smiles that communicated with ease & exactness. She wasn't threatened. But I didn't know if that made me feel good or bad. Then, without warning, Mary Lou sprung up from her seat, abruptly pushing her ice cream chair toward the bridge walkway as it made a screeching sound. Heads turned again. Announcing she was off to Undergarments, I followed dutifully leaving Jake to pay. I waved back to him for the second time that day.

It turned out to be unnecessary. He shadowed Mary Lou from department to department, and I think was glad when she finally decided on a pair of green gloves to match her skirt. I'd found my rock candy on the sixth floor and caught up with them as they waltzed slowly out the arcade's revolving doors.

"I can't wait to see the fountain," Mary Lou yelled back to let me know that's where we were headed next. I watched from behind, a bit resentful that Jake was playing tour guide instead of me.

Fifth Street Fountain sat in the middle of a long, narrow boulevard. Pigeons fluttered about and vendors hawked peanuts, hot dogs and frosty glass bottles of Cocoa Cola that clinked thickly the sounds of cool refreshment. Distant church bells chided us gently from the east. Twelve o'clock in Cincinnati. The three of us ambled toward the middle of the boulevard in the intense city heat. A merciless sun bore down upon the noon crowd drawing wavy mirages on cars that passed on either side of the fountain. We, like everyone else, gravitated to the showy display of water. Beads of sweat menaced Mary Lou's upper lip but only for a second or two. Plunging into her straw purse, she found the handkerchief of embroidery and lace that made her whole again with some patting. I watched her with great concentration as spewing water cascaded down into crescent-shaped pools then ascended in the form of swirling mists cooling our brows in delicious upward swells. The sky held its blue canopy over us like a magic incantation. Only one billowy cloud chanced on stage.

Beneath this limitless bright sky, Mary Lou focused her eyes intently on the grand lady of water. In a kind of pagan worship, they followed the outline of the ornate fountain that sported cherubs all around and the classic robed figure above. Then, as if directed from on high, she fell into a state of prayer. My face burned hot and I caught Jake's embarrassment as he looked around nervously. But her prayers were something I soon got used to.

Unlike Mary Lou, Jake wasn't so impressed, it seemed. While Mary Lou breathed in the misty air, he cast his eyes around, checking his watch, chewing the inside of his mouth.

"Hot," he muttered. "Really hot."

The bright, waving yellow gloves in the distance caught Mary Lou's attention. She walked toward them and we followed. It turned out to be Mary Lou's sixth-grade teacher who was shopping in the city for the day.

"This here's my beautiful sixth grade teacher I was tellin' you and aunty about the other night," Mary Lou exclaimed then paused looking back and forth from my face to her teacher's. "Patti Rae this is Miss Robins. Miss Robins, Patti Rae."

"How d'ya do," I said remembering to stand straight. I dutifully slipped my now tasteless piece of chewing gum under my tongue.

"This is my mother." Mary Lou's teacher nodded her head toward an older woman, and I saw the resemblance at once. Both possessed a strong jaw. That along with a slight upward sweep of the nose indicated their blood tie. I was reminded of my father's favorite saying: "Kentucky is a land of fast horses and beautiful women."

"Ya'll stayin' the night?" Mary Lou asked her teacher which I thought was a grown-up thing to ask. It made me take a look at Mary Lou in a different light.

"We're dining tonight at La Maison—we're meeting my uncle there. He works here in Cincinnati. And then we go on back down to Louisville tonight." The sixth grade teacher looked at her mother. "Won't we be dead tired when we get home!?" She winnowed out a short laugh and then blew a wisp of breath through her painted lips.

I noticed her vowels weren't held out as long as Mary Lou's and that she not only possessed beauty but a sense of showy fashion. The full noon sun that seared us, fell upon her kindly. Her lightly powdered skin stood strikingly pale against dark repeated waves that fitted upon her head like grasping hands. Her broad-brimmed hat seemed all wisdom in the heat. Watching its wide landscape as she turned her head this way and that, I was glad the elements had given this umbrella of sophistication a reason to come out.

We parted with gushing words and I was glad to be away from teacher and mother. The experience had seemed a strain.

"C'mon," Jake insisted.

Only after we'd taken our leave of Miss Robbins, did I realize Jake had not been introduced. Had he stepped away during our conversation or had Mary Lou purposely ignored him? I wondered. But I could see it didn't matter to Jake. His thoughts were somewhere else. Furrows had developed between his brows as if a great worry beat upon his mind in agonizing rhythms.

On our way to the RKO Albee Theatre, a destination I had proposed at the fountain, we passed the small but elaborate entrance to the Sheraton Gibson Hotel. Once again, Mary Lou stopped in urgent response to a new discovery.

"Well why dontcha look at that!"

"Wow!" I joined in. A white Rolls Royce pulled under a red and gold awning, emptying three gentlemen out its back door. "That's the most shiny car I've ever seen!"

"Not there!" Mary Lou shouted. Then she pointed just to the right of the chauffeured car. "Those guys with those little red pill box hats and red jackets to match! Not there. Over there! Have you ever?!"

There was so much commotion on the red-carpeted stairs of the hotel that it took me a while to realize it was the doormen and bellhops who were the object of Mary Lou's interest. One of the handsome bellhops winked at her, a gesture that brought out her easy giggle.

"How do ya keep those little hats on?" Mary Lou asked, barreling toward him swinging her crinolines with both hands. He lifted his hat better to reveal the black elastic strap that led under his chin. He smiled then looked around cautiously as if talking to a pretty girl was forbidden by management.

By this time, I was growing impatient.

"Mary Lou, we can't see everything. Come on! I'm gonna show you the prettiest building in Cincinnati. It's a movie house."

Jake agreed that we should take time to see a double feature while in town. He would join up with the guys again if we didn't mind.

"They're probably at Daelin's by now catchin' up on all the comic books," Jake stated casually eyeing his watch again. For Jake, it was as if something somewhere was diminishing like draining water with the passing of every minute.

"Do you have to go?" Mary Lou frowned. She didn't hide her disappointment.

But Jake didn't answer because he didn't hear. He was preoccupied with some force greater than himself, it seemed. I felt sure it wasn't his desire to meet up with the guys. Mary Lou must have sensed this also. For Jake found himself assuring her wrinkled face that he'd be waiting for us at the end of the double feature when we came out of the Albee. Then he was off in a fast trot before Mary Lou could protest further.

"Well!" She said forgetting the roses that now hung limp by her side.

CHAPTER 5

Walking the Halls

It was all I really wanted. Jake out of the picture. Things had been wearing on me. We were in Cincinnati against Mom's wishes. On top of that, it looked as though Mary Lou was falling for the only guy in town no one would approve of. But, suddenly, things were looking up. With Jake gone, Mary Lou's attention was there for the taking. I wanted it badly.

Having detoured to Sixth Street, we doubled back toward the Mecca of Cincinnati...the RKO Albee Theatre. It stood broad-shouldered and proud, crammed in between humbler buildings built earlier in the century. Edging slowly toward its pediment and columns, its classic beauty overshadowing all else, I watched Mary Lou to see her reaction. But there was nothing to indicate that the Theatre had yet registered. Nothing but a frown and what looked like a tumble of doubts. So I decided that patience was what I needed. I would gauge her face again once inside the Albee's stately halls.

"This is the RKO Albee Theatre! Ta da!" I announced proudly, arms akimbo. Behind me, the view of red-carpeted stairs and two lines of crystal chandeliers unfurled like a diamond necklace. There was a clattering of feet. They skirted around Mary Lou quickly. Three little boys in plaid suits and red bow ties led by their mother. Mary Lou had halted just inside the door, the bow ties almost running into her. I smiled. My patience had paid off. Transfixed, her gaze took in the high ceiling as tears pooled in her eyes. Giant posters of old Cincinnati stars like Tyrone Powers and Doris Day stared down at us from formidable walls that rose two stories high. Mary Lou and I were dwarfed by their imposing size and Hollywood glamour.

The dashing Zorro and petite blond watched as we disappeared into the great changeling halls that seemed theirs to protect and defend. I bounced all the way. Mary Lou floated.

"Two tickets please," Mary Lou laid out some change for both of us. The first feature was "The Seven-Year Itch" starring Marilyn Monroe. Cartoons were already playing, we were told. So, with tickets in hand, we hiked down a long hallway, stopping to buy popcorn before rushing to find the great auditorium. Not until we planted ourselves firmly into cushioned seats did we think to put the ticket stubs in our purses. I unsnapped mine, a boxy patent-leather affair, and threw the ticket in mindlessly. Mary Lou, with what seemed a solemn ritual, found one of two compartments in hers. She slipped the stub inside the pink straw box, her delicate fingers seeming to take note of its exact location. For a moment, her eyes were so intimately focused on something inside her purse that I imagined she could see Jake just beyond the clasp. It wouldn't have surprised me had she spoken to this phantom. But only a smile and a suspicious whisper escaped her lips. I, on the other hand, had had enough of Jake. I looked around at the old Vaudeville theatre that still sported its ancient red swags, jabots and box seats jutting out from the walls. I'd seen this auditorium many times but now, as earlier, I wanted to imagine it anew through Mary Lou's dreamy eyes.

"What are those pretty lights called on the walls?" Mary Lou asked as she plunged a careful hand into a cloud of popcorn.

"I don't know."

"Don't it seem just like Hollywood?"

"I guess it does." I brightened. She was starting to get it. "Yeah, it's probly just like Hollywood," I confirmed happily.

"And look at all those chandeliers," she exclaimed as she looked up.

"I hope they don't fall on our heads," I said watching her send up little prayers again. "They've probly been hangin' there for a thousand years. We better move." I pointed to a safety zone.

We sat through two features, laughing when other people laughed, though I didn't know why. And we applauded while the credits rolled even though it was to the screen only that we gave our approval.

When the lights came up, once again revealing the spectacle of an era gone by, the small afternoon crowd shuffled up the long aisles exiting in a slow march. We watched the shifting line of humanity as an extended part of the entertainment. Some comments volleying out from the crowd were hard to miss.

"Next time it gets hot, I'm puttin' my girdle in the freezer," a middle-aged lady confessed to the world. Immediately, I thought of my mother and her probable reaction to this vulgarity. She would have wilted in shock.

When I'd seen and heard enough and the soft cushioned seat grew hard beneath me, I gathered up my small purse and trash and stood to leave. Mary Lou, however, sat quietly in a sort of self-induced trance.

"This place makes me feel like a movie star," she said dreamily levitating out of her seat, her chin up and eyes swishing about beneath a haughty grin. She was pretending to be a movie star, I realized. So I did too.

We slid out of our aisle, out of the auditorium, and agreed that it would be fun to investigate Albee's old interior. With proprietary jaunts up and down wide stairwells leading to ante chambers and large rooms upstairs, we strode like models with heads back and eyes looking up into the high ceilings. Mary Lou swirled her crinolines, rustling them at people as they passed. In my awkward way, I mimicked her. I imagined us in gowns, silky and luxurious like the ones I'd seen in old black and white movies shown on Saturday mornings. When we passed the soft roar of a tall fan, our shimmering gossamer waved in a Hollywood breeze.

Down a broad and long stairwell off the main floor we discovered the Ladies Lounge. Here, ceilings soared over us in two-story splendor revealing cake-like decorations where wall and ceiling met. It was impressive by any standards. The series of ante-rooms leading to the lounge were like mirrored mazes. With a knowing smile, a lady in a black dress and starched full white apron, observed us keenly before telling us what she thought we should know. Standing straight and alert as a guard behind a dressing table of toilet water, hand lotion and linen towels, she provided an explanation for the twelve-foot mirrors. It turned out they were for nineteenth century skirt and petticoat adjusting when ladies' dresses were floor-length. The short sofas, she informed us, were called settees.

"These little couches here?" Mary Lou inquired with that upward lift of her southern drawl.

We admired the settees' tapestries depicting languorous women on ornate swings. I wondered where they could be. Was this a paradise on earth no one had yet told me about? Mary Lou ran her fingers across the smooth thick threads depicting spring-time scenes where flowers and perfect smiles sprang in perpetual bloom. But soon we were bored with the unique clutter of mirrored rooms and someone else's fantasy. We floated back up to the great halls that beckoned us, continuing our own fantasies and wandering about as if we belonged there.

I had just turned a dark and gloomy corner when, in a distant hallway, we heard a case clock chime.

"Oh my Gosh!" Mary Lou exhaled as if someone from behind had slapped her back. Then I remembered too.

"We almost forgot Jake!" I yelled out loud.

Without so much as a sigh, we forsook our imaginary gowns, movie stardom and the splendor of the old theatre. Our summer shoes softly pounding upon a continuous stream of red carpet, we passed chandelier after chandelier. There was no confusing this elegance with any other in Cincinnati, and I felt sad leaving it so abruptly. But I was happy in the thought that the RKO Albee was a place for all times. And for all times it would remain in the heart of Cincinnati. Were the intermittent chiming case clocks we heard in distant corners trying to tell us otherwise? It didn't matter. Meeting Jake pressed upon us as we flew through pleading hallways before reaching the front doors.

His casual pose in the shadow of the theatre's great awning seemed so Jake. With arms crossed, his shoulder lay casually against one of the columns that supported the entrance shelter. Its underside was now lit up by eight rows of round bright lights.

"How'd you like Marilyn?" He asked in a quiet murmur.

Mary Lou squeezed his arm and nodded quickly with enthusiasm, so pleased was she to see him.

"We had so much fun!" Mary Lou said taking my hand. But Jake wasn't in the mood to find out why.

"Now if you two don't mind, I'd like to walk you to Dixie Terminal and chaperone you back home." He was fidgeting with a battered square cigarette lighter the silver top of which he opened and closed with some concentration. There was a flinty scratch when he finally flicked it to light a short Camel's cigarette. Jake inhaled a sweet untainted aroma of tobacco before the smell reached my nose. It was only just for a second that I wished time could stand still. I was lulled into watching the art of his habit. The practiced inhale of it. The smoke hovered around us like a mysterious untold story. "...that is if you don't mind." He shifted his featherweight from one black boot to the other. "...I know your Mom wouldn't want you two over here by yourselves and..."

If time had stood still for me, it suddenly lurched forward. Without warning, Jake was cutting our day short by calling us up on our secret adventure.

"Jake," I said with some beginnings of anger.

He came forward with more authority in his voice. His head hung casually toward the ground and it seemed he was about to explain something to us by simply diverting his eyes.

"The reason why I think we oughta head on back is because...well, Buddy's Mom...somethin's happened."

"What happened," I asked wondering what he would come up with and figuring he was just trying to butt into my day.

"You know how Buddy's mom keeps close track of him?"

We all knew too well. I batted my eyes in impatience.

"She asked him to call home at 12:30 like she always does when we're out. And his Mom...she was all a mess."

"So?" Mary Lou asked. Her roses hung limply by an arm fully relaxed to her side, reflecting its owner's lack of interest.

"Sounds like somethin' bad's happened...about some strange man standing on her back porch just lookin' in at her and all. He scared her and when she screamed he just stood there, didn't move and she passed out... cold."

We were speechless.

"Buddy's Dad comes home at noon every day and found her lyin' on the floor in a daze," he continued. "Now, they can't keep her from cryin' and all and…well, she's the nervous type but still… it, it, it's just that we don't know who this guy is. So maybe we'd be just as well to get on home, you know?"

"But, Jake," I whined. "I'm not finished showin' Mary Lou around and all." His lips formed a new word for a new sentence but I interrupted. "Besides, looks like we'd be better off over here than at home."

"What about your Mom?" Jake intoned with what seemed real sincerity. It didn't matter. My mind was already running down a stubborn track.

"Don't you know that's probably just Spooky Lager's son who's not right in the head?" I surprised myself by thinking of this straight away. "He likes to look at women. Remember the time someone brought him to church and he didn't look up at the pastor but spent the entire sermon lookin' 'round at all the pretty women with his mouth wide open?" I was inspired by my own storytelling. "And after each song, he applauded 'cause he didn't know any better. And someone gave him some crayons and a coloring book and him 18 years old!"

"No." Jake said gazing up into a changing sky now billowing with clouds. "I never been to your church."

"Oh," I said. "That's right. I forgot." But I could see my explanation was good enough for Mary Lou.

"Come on with us!" She said grabbing Jake's arm. "Let's walk down Fourth Street. A sweet little old lady we met in the Powder Room just told us there's a garden on down here somewhere."

With a smile, finding consolation in Mary Lou's touch and my questionable rationale, Jake allowed himself to be led.

An unlikely trio, we glided down Fourth Street suddenly enjoying the day again. Inspired by our neighbor's unfortunate event, we playfully shuddered at the thought of ghouls and vampires that were the standard entertainment offered up to us on Saturday nights. Once Mary Lou shrieked with terror when Jake took off ahead of us then came bounding back as Frankenstein. When he saw he'd scared her, his long sinewy arm didn't take its chance to wrap itself around her. Instead, he stood quietly in front of Mary Lou with hands on her crossed arms. He asked her forgiveness as if he'd done something really bad.

I fell for Jake that very instant even though I tried to keep my feelings to myself. They were too busy peering into each other's eyes to notice me anyway. I mooned over Jake for weeks and wasn't even jealous that it was Mary Lou who had his attentions. But I vowed when I grew up, I'd go for a strong, silent type like Jake. Had I understood his kind was already a rarity, I would have dropped the whole project.

First we heard his mufflers. Then, like the feeling you get when credits come up on a movie you don't want to end, the handsome cop who'd chided us and had written down our names, came into view and pulled up alongside. The rumbling bike shook my brain.

"Somebody you picked up at the Fountain?" He asked with a crooked smile, directing his question to Mary Lou, not me. It didn't matter.

"Jake's a family friend," I blurted out too quickly. He laughed and so did Mary Lou. And, once again, I was left out.

But my childish response was vindicated. As the officer spun off, we heard him yell back sarcastically through the thundering noise. "Well, ya'll be caeful now, ya' hyea!"

Mary Lou turned chattering about something inconsequential to Jake whose teeth clinched and muscles tensed. The low groan issuing from his closed mouth was close to imperceptible but the expression on his face said it all. Anger. Then I heard her tell him not to worry about it.

We continued walking east on Fourth Street, first through a dense business district and then into an opening where hills, flowers, and the Ohio River converged into a perfect picture. In the midst of this idyll stood a tall bronze statue of a young, messy-haired Abraham Lincoln.

"I haven't never seen him before," I said looking up into his long and somber face.

"Look at that beautiful, long flower garden behind him, would you? Have you ever?" Mary Lou breathed. Then she quieted herself as she whispered silent prayers into the floral-scented air. Just beyond, a white federal-style mansion held dominion over Fourth Street's abrupt end. "The Taft Museum" was posted on a long wrought-iron fence that ran the length of the house. Its broad front yard stood at the end of the lush tract of flowers where the three of us took a bench that was overshadowed by a persimmon tree. Jake seemed so tired. It saddened me to sit and say nothing as we watched his concave chest heave in and out as if he were old and, unlike us, unable to take a summer heat. In an uncommon silence, I began to think about Mom. Surely Dad was home by now. But I couldn't be sure.

"Let's go," I dictated, grabbing Mary Lou's hand. "I think Jake wants to go home. So let's just go."

"I think that's a mighty fine idea," Mary Lou chimed. Then with no explanation, no expression of regret, she slid Jake's roses into a city garbage can sitting by the street corner. Jake looked at his roses in the can, then at Mary Lou. But he said nothing. Even if Jake could take the insult, I couldn't. So I ran back for them but Mary Lou called to me in a calm falsetto. "And how will we explain the roses to Aunty?"

We made for Dixie Terminal in a dirge of emotions. Jake held Mary Lou's hand and when she wasn't looking I saw it…his mournful eyes. They seemed to be asking the scores of people passing us by: "Will this dream ever be dreamed again?"

We walked at least fifteen blocks that day and I figured Mary Lou must have thrown around at least fifteen prayers. When Mom picked us up at the end of the car line—Jake had walked home—she saw the exhaustion in our faces and promised that supper would perk us up.

"How'd you like Covington, Mary Lou?" Mom asked, looking dwarfed in our green Pontiac as she drove nervously down our country road that followed DeCoursey Railroad Yards. Only about a mile out of the city, our valley's east hill directed us westward into our sleepy town and away from the noisy tracks of moving and disconnected rail cars.

"I liked the store with the perfume smells and the flying cans the best."

I smiled warmly at my cousin for saying this.

"Mom, how'd your day go?" I asked wondering if she'd heard about Buddy's mother.

"Just busy as always. Did some cannin'."

Mary Lou said, "Did you hear about…" But I grabbed her arm. If we told Mom about Bud's mother, she'd ask how we knew. I didn't want Jake's name to come up.

"Just let it slide," I whispered in Mary Lou's ear. I noticed then that her Evening in Paris had turned salty in a push of wind coming hotly through the cozy wings.

That evening I listened as Mary Lou fielded dangerously implicating questions about the day. Somehow it seemed Mom knew about our trip to Cincinnati but had decided to not make a fine point of it.

After dishes had been washed and stacked neatly into cupboards, Bob, Mary Lou, Mom, Dad and I adjourned to our side yard to get out of the suffocating heat of the kitchen. Cicadas scratched a familiar chant into the warm summer air. Over by the creek that followed the south perimeter of our property, tops of heads bobbed up and down behind a hill. My brother's friends. I pointed it out to Bob and shook my head.

"Idiots," I said.

Mom and I giggled.

In the early dusk, we watched Dad's cigar smoke hover in the air, phantom clouds changing shapes several times before disappearing. Mom and Mary Lou's legs moved in unison working the yard swing back and forth while Dad regaled us with some worn-out stories.

"What does the word 'chivalrous' mean?" Mary Lou questioned.

Surprised, Bob and I exchanged glances.

"You ever read King Arthur?" Dad inquired.

We took Dad's broad vocabulary and reading for granted. We assumed all fathers possessed his command of the English language. We also assumed all the stories he entertained us with were heard by all kids our age in their homes. We never understood, until years later, this was not the case. The tree frogs revved into full symphony and mosquitoes made dangerous sorties through Dad's cigar smoke which he blew continually our way to keep the snipers at bay.

All the excitement of the day finally caught up with me. My eyes grew heavy as Dad's voice slowly changed its sound and tenor as if travelling through a long tunnel. Behind us, the woods loomed dark and the night birds' calling echoed. As I took for granted I would always have Mom and Dad back then, I also assumed the woods would always be there as well. It was an important part of our lives…the sharp cedar smells, the sounds, always inviting us into its mysteries, proprietary as the sky.

And, just as important as the woods, there was Francis. A friend of friends who seemed perennially to walk its paths. It was his favorite place in the world, he said. I saw him right after we came in from town. Standing by the edge of the woods, I caught sight of him trimming summer's tangle of weeds that encroached on our property. I ran to him, anxious to share the dreadful story of Von Stroben. I could tell Francis anything and not have to worry that he would tell my mother.

He said, in his quiet way, not to bear Von Stroben "ill will." That some people do things out of lonliness…that I should only feel love for such people as well as sympathy. But that I should not believe everything everyone says, either, especially if too many compliments are given. "Beware of Greeks bearing gifts," he announced standing straight and in a dramatic pose. "But always be kind," he said falling back to an at-ease posture. "You can always say 'no, thank you.'"

It all made sense, in a strange sort of way, except that he said it would help me live a fuller life if I did this. If I loved this man. If I could forget the ugly and remember how he seemed part of the time he talked. Good always comes out of any conversation, Francis said. He said you just have to listen for it. But how could I love a man like Von Stroben? I wondered if anyone could after being so cruelly tricked as Mary Lou and I had been. But there was something I admired about him and maybe that was the good Francis referred to. I reasoned it probably had nothing to do with his character. Perhaps it had to do with his imagination. It was that glimmer of contagion I had felt on the sidewalk next to him, not the thing that made him feel powerful but his creating it out of nothing.

"Basically," Francis exhaled and then inhaled as if some new thought were lamentable. "There are those among us who have little to offer in terms of love or friendship…we are the lonliest and perhaps know there is very little within us that can attract the love we so badly need."

Francis picked up a dead stick, sliding it against an old stump, ridding it of a slick black that had formed up and down its length.

"…so we lay in wait like a spider and grab the first prey that presents itself easily enough on our web."

He wasn't looking at me any more and seemed to be talking to himself.

"We sting, paralyze then devour. In other words, we control."

I looked at Francis not really understanding everything. Just some things.

From below we heard Mary Lou's giggle.

"Did your cousin cry after the spider pounced on her?" Francis inquired changing the tenor of his voice.

"Not really," I chuckled, thinking he was being funny. "To be honest, it didn't seem to bother her at all. A really handsome cop took down our names and everything on a piece of paper and she just started talkin' to him like she… she was flirting really," I chirped.

"Really?"

"Yeah, she didn't seem upset at all."

"Excellent." Francis said, watching Mary Lou in our yard below. She was dancing around my mother who was trying, without much success, to hang bed sheets on a clothesline.

From the top of the hill Mary Lou looked and acted just like any other young girl my age. Francis laughed to himself.

"Patti Rae," he stated calmly. "I think your cousin's going to be good for you."

But all I could think of was Von Stroben and how different he was from my dear old friend, Francis. I loved Francis and was content to make him feel I'd do anything he said. Insofar as Von Stroben was concerned, it took me years to forgive him.

As I lay upon the dusk-wet grass pondering the day's events, just for an instant I thought I heard someone behind me. I jerked around quickly to find no one there. But I felt and saw the shadow go over me.

CHAPTER 6

Moon Flowers

Gasping for air. Waking out of the black of subconsciousness. The noise that had jerked me from my sleep continued…

"Bump, bump, bump, bump, bump," it began faintly. Then a louder and faster "bump, bump, bump, bump, bump, bump, bump, bump, bump!" I fell back onto my pillow sighing in relief. It was, after all, a familiar sound. Connecting freight trains just two hills over, echoed into the warm lap of our valley.

Looking up through my window, losing myself in the indigo blue of a quiet sky where a host of stars made their usual patterns. In their midst the moon hung confidently, over-protective and full-faced. I imagined it had awakened me. Its pocked smile peered through my bedroom window like a mother's watch and bathed the foot of Mary Lou's bed in silvery light. Earth smells wafted gently through the air from the dark outside. Running close by our house, a creek teamed with a community of snails full-stretched from their concentric shells. Nocturnal creatures walked about shaking their summer furs, leaving primal musk in the damp night air. And there was that other smell, ambrosial, something I considered a miracle of the night. I wondered if I imagined it or if its ghostlike fragrance had somehow, through the moonlit grayness, found its way into our den of sleep. Unlike popsicles or cold sweet watermelon treats on hot summer days, the beauty of the moonflowers was a luxury too mysterious, too special to run after too often. Maybe only once or twice in the summer would I visit it in its nightly lair. With a certainty, I knew this was one such night. This miracle and Mary Lou belonged together.

Touching Mary Lou's shoulder gently, I whispered, "Wake up, Mary Lou." I felt badly when she bolted to a sitting position.

"What's wrong?"

"The moonflowers," I said sheepishly.

"Moonflowers?"

"Yeah. Can you smell 'em?" I was surprised at her smile that broadened slowly but into something sure, full of warmth and a knowing. Some people have the ability to convey volumes through their eyes. I've never forgotten hers just then out of their nascent sleep. They indicated that, despite the four-year difference in our ages, perhaps we were soul mates after all.

"Where are they?" She slumped back upon her pillow. "And what are they?"

"In Mrs. McCullough's wood-side garden, in full bloom right about now."

She turned her head with some question and smiled again, willing to hear more.

"They only bloom at night and only in the light of the moon. We've got to hurry," I whispered coarsely, checking the buttons on my pajama top. I could see I had a willing partner when she yawned, then dragged the palm of her hand under my bed feeling for her slippers. She found only a ballerina doll I'd forgotten to put away before her visit.

Still in our pajamas, we padded our bare feet down a narrow path that led behind white and yellow frame houses on our side of the valley. Mary Lou giggled at our new adventure and twice I heard her whisper "moonflowers". The moon's smug grin had disappeared behind a solitary cloud giving many stars in our vision full stage. Practiced in the art of sky watching, I caught a glimpse of a star falling from the sky.

"Catch a falling star and put it in your pocket," I sang off-key then snatched the imaginary star mid-air with a practiced flourish. I showed Mary Lou how one can easily put a star in the breast pocket of a pajama top and save it for a rainy day. But as was her habit, she had embraced just one idea, the moonflowers, seeming to mount some unusual hope upon hope, nothing else mattering at that moment.

"Moonflowers," Mary Lou whispered again, confirming her willingness to be led into the shimmering half-light of my fantasy world.

We began our climb after crossing over Mr. Babcock's creek bridge. Approaching the edge of Mrs. McCullough's woods, I saw it was suffused in dim ivory light. The moonflowers were just as I had described. Standing at perfect attention in their nightly glade, their vines crept upward along a makeshift trellis, soft and dewy. Mary Lou walked cautiously up to their delicate blossoms as if they would drop at her approach. I never asked Mrs. McCullough if she chose this spot for planting by sitting up late at night calculating lunar movement. But something like that must have happened.

Mary Lou sniffed and touched the night blossoms with studied care. It was as if she wanted to make sure they weren't part of a dream from which she was yet to awaken. Prepared for the prayer I felt sure would escape her lips, I moved to one side not wanting to interfere with its upward draft. A moment long in silence reminded me of church and the many fervent prayers sent up when something crucial to our fellowship had happened. Besides a slight rustling in the woods that carried a hard, almost human sound—perhaps a lone rabbit or deer come down to sniff the sweetness—it was a somber moment as if the world had stopped. Beauty in the night. Mary Lou and the evanescent moonflowers.

Then there was that sudden creak of a door that I still hear sometimes when my days fill up with modern phantoms. Our heads turned in the same direction.

Mary Lou shrieked. I jerked up from the ground.

Our eyes trained on Mrs. McCullough standing straight and defiant at her back door. The shotgun she held expertly, pointed to our heads.

"Mrs. McCullough! It's me, Patti Rae!" I screamed.

The gun dropped from a shooting position.

"Do Jesus!" A disgusted Mrs. McCullough called out. Then she mumbled something to herself, barely audible to our ears. It was clear she was not pleased. As she walked up the hill toward us, I saw that a recent fear had left her face like a flood that leaves a creek bed muddy. The shotgun dangled over her right arm and a smile made its way past waning anxiety. "Admiring my moonflowers, are ya?"

"Yes ma'am."

"Well, how long do you plan to walk about? Sakes alive, you shoulda answered me the first time."

"What first time, Mrs. McCullough?" I asked confused.

"Why the first time I yelled out and asked who was there when you were snoopen' round my front door! That's what first time!"

Mary Lou pleaded without being introduced, "We just got here ma'am, I can swear that, we just got here this very minute."

"This is my cousin Mary Lou," I said, smiling, but an old fear receded, once again pressed upon Mrs. McCullough's face. She ignored the introduction with uncharacteristic bad manners, abruptly shoving the shotgun under her right arm. She grabbed our hands with authority, us giving no resistance, pulling Mary Lou and me down her back yard as we stumbled behind her. I was intrigued by the sudden drama.

"Mrs. McCullough? What's the matter?"

She said nothing until she had pulled us through the back door of her white two-story that was the largest home in our neighborhood.

"Someone's been out there for nigh an hour," she said once inside her dark kitchen. The lights were off so she could peer out the windows undetected.

"We didn't see no one comin' over," I countered. "Probly just some kids staying up late to play in the woods."

"No Patti Rae. This was not the noise of kids. It was a snooping noise, like someone was trying to be quiet but doesn't know where my loud flowers are."

"Oh."

"I thought I saw a shadow through my bedroom screen window too. That's what woke me up. And I think it stood there for a while looking in... too tall to be ole Dugan," Mrs. McCullough said fidgeting with her unpinned hair, implying that we had a Dracula or something otherworldly prowling our neighborhood. "Whoever it is that's playing peepin' Tom in this town is sure havin' a field day. But, I swear, if it comes around again, it's gonna pay! No faintin' around here!"

I was pretty sure Mrs. McCullough was referring to Bud's mother who had passed out the day before and it was our first indication someone else in the neighborhood had heard about her scare. I figured if she knew, everyone else did too. That included my own mother who obviously had decided to keep this "peeping Tom" news from Mary Lou.

The fear that had grown inside Mrs. McCullough for the hour she'd been alone, now broke out in quick, nervous gestures the energy of which took root in Mary Lou and me.

"Most likely it's Dugan's boy. Him and his dark clothes. He's gonna get caught one of these days, you just wait and see. A little jail time wouldn't do him no harm, that's for sure. Take the starch outta him lickety split."

Mary Lou and I stood holding each other trembling and suddenly cold. My shoeless feet had taken on a purple cast and my fingertips grew numb.

While checking and re-checking her deceased husband's shotgun, Mrs. McCullough peered out all the windows from front to back, pulling at her sacred drapes that I now realized bore uncanny resemblance to the ones we saw the day before at the RKO Albee Theatre. You could see the dust shake out from not having been handled much.

Mrs. McCullough mumbled to herself as she put on the teapot. We learned from her half sentences and one-sided conversation that we were to stay there for the rest of the night. "Too dangerous these days for a soul to be out in her own yard!"

I watched Mary Lou for some reaction to the condemnation of Dugan's boy but then realized Mary Lou didn't know that Dugan's boy was Jake. She seemed only sympathetic to the situation and Mrs. McCullough's fear.

"Where's her husband?" Mary Lou whispered in my ear.

"He died. She's a widow lady," I said wondering how many nights Mrs. McCullough had spent like this since the passing of her short, pot-bellied husband. We all missed Mr. McCullough. During Halloween, the loss was felt more bitterly. The McCullough's had been, up until his death, my and everyone else in the neighborhood's favorite stop for begging. Sometimes a white-sheeted ghoul, sometimes a vampire, Mr. McCullough welcomed you through the door of his home, flashlight under chin, into his "laboratory". Once convinced he'd thoroughly scared the wits out of us, the lights came on. With a flash of his white sheet, or bat wing, a candied apple was shoved into our faces. Peals of laughter rang out from their house at Halloween sustaining our community's life force in the face of impending winter. Mr. McCullough was known for his kindness, but God help the trespasser or drunk from our neighborhood saloon found snooping in his yard or his wife's flower garden. His gun was never for show.

"You'll sleep in the hide-a-bed if you don't mind," Mrs. McCullough spoke softly now, carefully placing her deceased husband's gun in the hallway.

So we followed her to the front parlor after taking our chamomile tea in nervous gulps. She pulled at a lower panel of the sofa with a great heave. The hide-a-bed reared up in a hump and a bang and, to my surprise, was already encased in floral sheets and pillowcases. Mary Lou gazed in awe at the handsome furniture she may have never seen the likes of before. Though dark, there was enough street light through the windows that glinted off the richly shellacked secretary and cherry occasional tables revealing a luster of handsome wood and strange symmetry of tracings. There were vases behind glass and beautiful figurines sat around everywhere waiting to be broken. Mom always said "Poor Mrs. McCullough. Childless and lonely." I wondered if her pretty things were any consolation. I hoped so. But the house smelled stale, like old people. And something hung about the old varnish odors and sweetish floral scents coming out from every corner evolving into an altogether complete picture. Monotony.

"There," Mrs. McCullough said turning back the sheets. "Whoever's been snoopin' about surely must have been scared off by now. Let's all get some sleep."

She said goodnight, patting our heads which was as much affection as a neighbor should show, I figured. Then turning with a more relaxed look on her face and holding her white gown in a knot to one side, she ambled into a large room where a funereal four-poster bed awaited her lonely rest. I decided I was glad we had come out to see the flowers. Without us, Mrs. McCullough may have not gotten much sleep.

Unfortunately, oval portraits of frowning ancient people garbed in dark suits and the soft pitter patter sounds behind the floral papered walls kept me from getting any sleep. And I was so tired. Around 4:00 a.m., I had to use the bathroom but was afraid to get up, afraid that if I knocked something over, it would kill Mrs. McCullough. I chose to stay in bed.

Mrs. McCullough woke us up before Thurston Pile's rooster had a chance to crow. I wondered aloud why we hadn't heard Mr. Shortcakes.

"That's because it's only five o'clock." Mrs. McCullough explained and helped us out of bed hurriedly so that the most important order of the day could be accomplished. Making the bed. We helped her push it back under the divan after watching her strain at the corners creating perfect tucks and applying smoothing swipes to her floral sheets. She moved like a farm wife as if it were necessary to keep pace with the milking of cows, the canning of vegetables and every angle of the sun that ran warmly through summer like a proverbial hare. With brisk, quick movements, she served up bacon, eggs, toast and orange juice from her wood's side kitchen. Watching us eat like any doting mother, she insisted every morsel was consumed and remarked upon.

"Those are mighty big eggs, Mrs. McCullough," I crowed thinking a compliment might smooth the furrows between her delicate gray brows.

"Well, they should be," she chuckled. "They come from Thurston Pile's hen house where no hen could be happier."

With another maternal pat on the head, she sent us traipsing cautiously across the path we'd followed the evening before in the pink gray dimness of a new dawn. It occurred to me that it was still fairly dark outside and ominous shadows fell backwards from familiar landmarks giving them an unfamiliar cast. But I was sure Mrs. McCullough knew best. If there was anyone about that night, they surely must be gone by now. Which was why, while passing behind the same cottages with still darkened windows, I was surprised to hear footsteps behind us. Maybe Mrs. McCullough running after us with something we left behind. So I stopped. Mary Lou stopped too. We looked but no Mrs. McCullough. No one. A fog had risen from the east creek giving us only a few yards of clear vision. We waited to see if anyone emerged from its gray mists. When Mr. Shortcakes crowed again, we jumped, then clinched hands darting away from the mists and charging quickly past the rock wall that introduced our property from the north. It's jutting surface embraced riots of honeysuckle vines that had heard the call of summer and were beginning to bud. When we turned the corner of our house, we stopped abruptly, unnerved again, looking behind us first, then toward the light shining out from our kitchen. The sound was hideous in the early morning quiet, as startling as a pack of wolves crying into the night. It lurched out through our kitchen screen door. Sorrowful crying in sudden stops and starts sending cold shivers down my body.

"He's never home at night anymore!"

We slipped back behind a lilac bush so my mother couldn't see us through the screen door. It was an old bush laboring under the strain of purple blossoms. The intense fragrance made me dizzy.

"What am I going to do?!"

I recognized our next door neighbor's voice. Mrs. Samuels must have had another bad night. I could imagine Mom sitting there listening because Mom said that's what good neighbors do. She was trying her best to convince Mrs. Samuels that most of her anxieties were brought on by her own imagination. But that seemed to only make matters worse.

"You don't know what it's like. You have the perfect husband." Her cries continued mournfully making the hair on my arms stand up. "He's always home at night and you never have to worry about grocery money. And he goes places with you…to church and you know. Mine…" her words trailed off into groaning sobs.

The tale of woe continued as we yawned and settled against one of Dad's many rock walls. We agreed we'd sneak back upstairs once Mrs. Samuels left and Mom went to another room. At this high point and with the fog lifted, we could see Mr. Tate letting his cows out of the barn. They were black dots moving slowly on the other side of the valley on the east hill. His dog was a fast speck snipping at the cows. Its faint barking in the distance trailed over to our side of the valley in echoing waves.

But what would she do if she divorced her husband, was the argument now trailing out to our tired ears.

"Well, you know," Mom said, her voice hiking up at the end to make a positive note. "You could get a job at the Five and Dime serving up candy." I could hear Mom's chair screeching closer to our neighbor's. "I heard just this week that Ruthie Watkins…you know Ruthie. She used to play the organ at All-Saint's Church…"

"I don't think I know her," our neighbor said in a sad voice.

"Well, you poor thing. Don't you ever buy yourself candy when you go to town?" But Mom didn't wait for an answer realizing, too late, it was a badly chosen question. "Well what she does is, is she shovels chocolates, peanuts and candies into little white bags. Now she's leaving her job to marry one of the managers that she met there and…well, I don't know why you couldn't do that job. It'd be awful pleasant, dontcha think?"

If Mom had anticipated a bright response, she was surely disappointed. The suggestion sent Mrs. Samuels into another crying jag as she imagined what her mother would think. She, divorced and working. She viewed her life on this one canvass of disgrace at which point, louder wailing resumed. Three menacing minutes passed, the end of which Mrs. Samuels found her center of calm and the crying ceased except for a few intermittent quakes and whimpers. Then, as logic displaced hysteria, they discussed how Mrs. Samuels might horde some money away for those times when her husband's drinking had taken it all. And in a more realistic vein, Mom suggested what to do when her husband came home drunk; what she might be able to do with her son whose handicap allowed him the barest facility for feeding and clothing himself but that was about all. It sounded pretty desperate to me but I was too tired to care much. I told Mary Lou, who looked surprisingly sad, not to worry.

"This happens all the time."

But tears fell from her eyes as I stupidly elaborated on many other past calamities visited upon Mrs. Samuels. Soon, it was as if Mary Lou's tears jumped into my eyes but I blinked them away quickly

"She'll feel better after a while and then everything'll be okay again. You'll see."

Soon lack of sleep caught up with us as we listened to the humming voices inside and as the sun peered cautiously over the eastern hill sending its strands of gold down through our little valley. For the third time in eight hours, we fell asleep but now in a close knot for warmth.

We might have slept like that for a while but a feathered Casanova at the edge of town, practiced in the art of human awakenings, shrilled out yet another cocka doodle doo! Mr. Shortcakes. Startled, we awoke to see Dad and his best friend, Gilbert, trudging up the walk that followed the side of our house. We were too immobilized by sleep to move.

"What are you girls doin' out so early?"

"We, uh, we went up to the tree house to get a book I wanted to show Mary Lou."

"This early? Usually you sleep in on Saturdays. Where's the book?"

"Uh, I don't know." I said lifting my shoulders. "It's not there anymore."

"Well, get on inside. We'll have your Mom fix some pancakes this morning."

Gilbert, grunting as if I were heavy, pulled me up by my arms. "Come on, squirt." Gilbert liked to coddle, not just me, but all kids under thirteen years of age in our neighborhood. As Mayor of Jefferson, he said it was his duty. He and his wife were childless but only in the technical sense. Their home was as familiar to us as our own. What with caged parakeets in the solarium, and cats everywhere to make us worry about the parakeets, it was full of adventures and temptations hard to resist. A continual chirping issued from their white two-story through the day while kids ran out with their pockets filled with candy or ran in bearing wild flowers. Gilbert's wife liked to see fresh wildflowers on her kitchen table and had a special crystal vase in which to display all those brought to her. The constant movement of children in their home was testament to the love she and Gilbert parceled out freely and got back in abundant return.

"Ouch!" I yelled.

"What's wrong?" He had grabbed my hand but now let it drop.

"I think I got a splinter or somethin'."

Gilbert bent over my finger with a serious look. His glasses dropped to the tip of his aquiline nose. "Well now. Let's have a look-see."

I tried to yank my hand out of his giant grip but was powerless.

"S'just a little hair of a thing. Have your Mom wrap it in bacon. That and a little hug oughta do it." Then Gilbert hugged me carefully seeing that I probably needed that more than bacon. There was brute strength in his tall, stocky frame that he reigned in delicately around children. Hugging was his favorite gesture. It was an unusual male trait in those days and is what made him enormously popular.

Before Dad opened the back door, he turned to us looking unusually grave.

"We got something to tell you and your mother and brother," Dad rasped in an acrid tone. He hadn't included Mary Lou. I looked at her but she was too sleepy to notice. "Get on in here."

The screen door banged in turn as each of us entered the kitchen. I imagined a powwow would ensue immediately. Maybe Mrs. McCullough had told Dad about our evening escapade. Or maybe he found out about our trip to Cincinnati. I expected nothing short of a finger-pointing lecture. But when Dad and Gilbert glimpsed Mrs. Samuel's red face and eyes to match, they made a practiced detour to the basement.

"Boo hoo hoo!" Her cries followed them down the stairs.

Good old Mrs. Samuels, I thought to myself, has saved me. But I was convinced this was only a postponement, so took the opportunity to do whatever I could in my power to soften what was sure to come.

I ducked my head through the basement door and saw Dad and Gilbert talking over a pile of wood, tools and frog-gigging harpoons. "Hey Dad, what are you 'n Gilbert doin' up so early? Goin' fishin'?" I smiled broadly as if it were my heart's desire that he have fun. Before he could answer, my brother came dashing down from upstairs. Rushing through the dining room, Bob slid, almost falling as he made his customary sharp turn at the table. There was an astute recovery then he pushed me away from the basement door.

"What happened?" Bob asked like he knew something was up.

"Sure enough, ole Babcock was right, Bob," Dad rasped again looking up past a naked light bulb. "A woman was killed in a woods down by the railroad yards. They found her last night."

Gilbert whispered something in Dad's ear we couldn't hear, then Dad continued. "Mrs. Butler's sister who was visiting from Cincinnati...they said she was out picking wild berries. Poor thing." There was an almost imperceptible break in his voice. "They'd been looking for her all yesterday. Found her with her tin pail of berries spilled out everywhere and mingled..." Gilbert touched Dad's arm and that was the end of the story.

"Who killed her?" Bob asked.

"We don't know."

"How'd she get killed?" Bob pushed.

"You don't need to know, son."

Bob announced the news to Mom and Mrs. Samuels and that finished their conversation. Shock supplanted Mrs. Samuel's desperation with a morbid relief and the murder was the topic of discussion for the remainder of the day.

After forcing down pancakes—we kept our little midnight rendezvous with the moonflowers to ourselves—Mary Lou and I dressed and flew back across the path we'd taken earlier in the morning. We had to tell Mrs. McCullough right away. We had to tell her she hadn't imagined the noises or the hulking shadow. But her next door neighbors beat us to it.

We found her on the divan inhaling smelling salts. Mrs. Truthers and Miss Molly George, both dressed in cotton smocks, had propped her head up from a lying position and patted her hands. Mrs. Truthers, Jefferson's most proficient town gossip, sing-songed, "You must have a thousand guardian angels watchin' over you, is what I say."

We left.

CHAPTER 7

A True Friend

"Hold on just a minute! I don't want you up in that woods! Get back down here!" Mom yelled out the back door, catching us only a few feet from its brambled edge. We were so close, we could see wild fern and small-capped mushrooms that pushed up through dark loam.

The timing of the murder couldn't have been worse. That day I had planned to take Mary Lou into the solemn mysteries of the woods where I'd introduce her to the world I loved most. A world of deep green moss and bright glades that moved when the wind caught the trees above.

"You heard what your Mom said," Mary Lou protested. "Let's just sit here in the yard or go back and see the moonflowers again."

Wasn't good enough for me. So I rationalized with a doubtful Mary Lou.

"I don't know who the murderer is, but he'd be plum crazy to come up this far. There's not a minute goes by but what there's not maybe two or three of us comin' and goin' in here." I indicated our back woods with a flippant wave of my hand.

Mary Lou still looked doubtful.

"If we screamed only just once, why, every mom and dad would be up here in a flash." I snapped my fingers confidently.

We cut across the small creek and approached the entrance to the woods from the south so Mom wouldn't see us. The entrance was like a church foyer and considered the best by most kids in Jefferson. Like a church, it was the location of many of our furtive meetings. Polio drives started here. Ideas for the latest jitney design were discussed beneath its canopy. Cabbage night pranks were agreed upon in this solemn spot and it was the best place to find out the latest on who beat up whom. Its shape was circular and at its center stood an ancient tree. A large hole notched into this tree's base was believed by neighborhood kids to be domiciled by bears in the winter even though bears had never been seen in our part of the state. It was an easy tree to climb and held precariously, with its old branches, one of the oldest and best lookout tree houses in the neighborhood.

From the "foyer", smaller wood paths branched out. One ran south to the creek whose wider beds bore the full brunt of run-off from the top of the hill during the spring. Another led directly west up the steep cliffs which was sort of like Main Street. From there, smaller arteries led to various points of interest. There was a less worn path we called the "Avenue of the Witch Trees" that led cautious travelers through its winding groves of snarled and angry-looking Hawthorns and thorny bushes. The short serpentine path was my favorite. Various specimens of wild flowers grew like delicate children along the way, depending upon the seasons: Blue Bells and Dutchmen's Britches in the spring, Flox and Columbine in the summer. Or there was the path that led you perilously up the steepest cliffs leading to the western-most edge of the woods where, in the early spring, its tender yellow charge of daffodils bloomed like laughter. The most traveled path led to a precipice of hanging grapevines that had been cut by ambitious teenagers. Their long peeling arms offered short trips over an abrupt escarpment. Longer, more dangerous swings brought the young trees from below into view. With the tip tops of these, many of us had made acquaintance when older vines weakened and dropped us gently to the ground. The path leading directly north stayed close to the eastern edge of the woods and was a quick way to move to a neighbor's house under the cloak of dense vines and undergrowth.

"Which path will we take this morning?" Mary Lou asked after this introduction, now seeming to forget or not caring any longer about present dangers.

"Let's follow the creek up the hill for several yards. The last spring rains formed a pretty pool just a ways up. I've put shells around it that we brought back from Florida last year. It's a shell wonderland."

"A shell wonderland?"

Mary Lou kept pace with me, tripping only twice over tree roots that jutted out like octopus tentacles. She soon learned to keep her vision downward toward these snarling traps, obstacles of no burden to me, so well had I memorized each inch of every path.

It was a relief to see the pool had not been tampered with by varmints or looted by the McGuffey boys. They were a strawberry blond set of brothers, four doors down, who did spiteful things to girls' dolls or anything "girl" left in the woods. A churlish father, outraged often by his small, timid wife, encouraged their belief that the woods was their domain, not girls'.

"Where did the pearls come from?" Mary Lou asked spying them in the joints of propped open shells.

"Mom gave me one of her old necklaces."

"Are they real?"

"I guess. But some of 'em are peeling." Then I told her about the day I put all of this together: my old Tiny Tears dipping her toes in the water, the star fish I put next to a pile of costume jewelry that looked like a pirates' stash, the conch shells positioned at studied angles. I told her how one afternoon I hid behind a log nearby when I heard the McGuffey boys approaching.

"Sure enough they came sniffin' around kickin' my things in the creek and I told 'em if they didn't stop, I'd shoot 'em with my BB gun. They just laughed 'cause they know Mom & Dad won't let us use a BB gun 'cept for target practice. But Francis, my best friend, came along and he scared 'em off."

Mary Lou laughed deep inside her throat and suggested that, some day, I would be more interested in boys than conch shells and that I'd get married and have babies. I looked out into the calm pool with its unlikely shell display. It was funny how just those few words herded me into a place that seemed closed in and stale even though I sat under a green canopy of familiar woods.

"What's wrong, Patti Rae?"

"I was thinkin' of how they never come to the woods or stay out late enough to chase lightening bugs. And when do ya ever see 'em laying on their back looking up into the sky?"

"Who?"

"They miss the wild flowers every spring," I continued in my own thoughts. "And if you ask 'em to come up and see 'em they say they're too busy."

"Who's they?" Mary Lou asked again picking up a long necklace from the pirate's stash.

"Any woman who gets married it seems. How come they stay in the house most of the time?" I asked Mary Lou, hoping she'd have a reasonable answer. "All they think about are their pressure cookers and how many white towels they can pull out of a detergent box."

"Well there's nothin' wrong with that," Mary Lou offered her own brand of logic as her eyes followed the sound of a nightingale. She looked strangely hopeful, as if the feathered visitor had the power to drop something magical from its throat.

"Crimony! They spend all their day folding towels just so. Mom thinks sittin' at her roller iron watching the sheets go in wrinkled and coming out smooth is important. Just looks boring to me."

"She wants to make sure you have everything nice. That's all, Patti Rae."

"But, your mom. She's different. I remember how, the last time we came down to visit, how she got out in the early mornin' and talked to the birds and rabbits…and one time…do you remember this…she came out to help us make bracelets out of clover in your front yard."

"I don't remember that. But I do know your mom's got more to do closer here to the big city. We live on a farm. We don't have to worry about such things. Nobody cares, really. But here, you gotta have things nice 'n all."

"But my mom comes from a farm too and…" I couldn't continue because I really couldn't put together what it was I wanted to say. But then a thought occurred to me that seemed appropriate.

"All mothers around here come from farms, if you ask 'em. What makes 'em change?"

"Well, they have babies to take care of, children and husbands to feed, laundry to do, houses to keep pretty and all that stuff that makes 'em wives." Mary Lou looked at me sideways. "You know what I mean." She shifted her weight and dropped one foot into my decorated creek pool. "They're adults and that's what adults around here do and what they like to do."

"Then I think I'll stay like this the rest of my life. I don't see no reason to change and, if I do change, I don't think I want to have all that. Don't it seem boring to you?"

Mary Lou sighed. "All I know is I want to fall in love and marry a handsome man who'll take care of me and my children so we can live happily ever after." Then she added after a few seconds, "…and I'll take care of him. But I'll go gathering berries right alongside my children—there'll be about five of 'em—and I'll teach 'em how to ride horses and we'll have a woods just like this in the back of our house, and we'll make little play pools the way you have here." Mary Lou waved her hand over my creation. "And my husband won't be just any husband, you know."

"No?" I said, interested in what that meant.

"No. He'll have to be a special person…not just any ole man."

"Like what kind of man will he be?"

"Good looking, of course. Fun. He should have a good job so we can have a big house for our kids. You know, stuff like that. But I guess most of all, he'll like the same things I do."

"Like what?" I said wondering if men and women could like the same things.

"Like…well, you know. He'll like horses and he'll like pickin' flowers by a creek and sittin' in the grass and watchin' the clouds." Her voice trailed off. "You know. Just like you said."

I tried to think of anybody's father who did stuff like that. For the life of me, I couldn't.

Then I considered that maybe she hadn't really understood the conversation in Mom's kitchen that morning. Maybe one conversation like that wasn't enough. Maybe she needed to hear a lot of conversations like that or just bickering between one's own mom and dad. Or maybe she needed to see a mother sad and lonely sometimes-- that marriage is not a fairy tale, not like the woods.

"What next?" Mary Lou asked, seeing I might be a little disgusted with her views.

"Well, if we're real quiet, we might be able to hear him in the distance. Or if we start screamin' a little bit, he'll think something's wrong and come to see."

"Who is he, Patti Rae?"

"My best friend who loves the woods... even though he's an adult." I smiled at my own remark.

She looked at me skeptically, but I was used to that.

"He has a beautiful white beard, long hair, wears woolen trousers, a vest and jacket. He's so cute with his funny little hat and he always carries a walking stick. Says it helps him along life's paths."

"Patti Rae, who is this guy, really?"

"He's just a nice old man who likes to walk in the woods. Seems like nobody else sees him but me. But that's okay..."

Mary Lou looked horrified, but I continued.

"You should hear him sometimes. He recites poetry and..."

"Patti Rae, you can't be serious! What you're telling me is that...what you're...you're talking about a man who could be the murderer!"

"The murderer?" I couldn't believe my ears. "Francis? Not Francis." And I smiled to get her to see. "Francis is just the opposite of a murderer, silly. He helps people. He wouldn't hurt a flea. He's the best friend I ever had!"

"So where does Francis live?" Mary Lou asked abruptly with deep breaths indicating the benefit of a doubt.

"Well," I tried to remember what he'd told me. "He lives up on the highway at the top of this hill." I pointed west. "But I think he spends more time in the woods. He really likes the woods," I said imagining I could paint a picture that adequately described his loveliness.

But the effect was just the opposite. In a gesture of shock that both confused and irritated me, Mary Lou grabbed my hand and dragged me out of the woods and back down our yard. It was the second time that day someone had dragged me from a place I loved.

"Mary Lou, stop it. You're ruining it. Wait a minute!" Her grip was hard and final and it hurt my hand. We burst through the back door into Mom's steamy kitchen.

"Aunt Martha!" Mary Lou breathed the words out heavily just four inches from my mother's face.

After condemning Francis without ever having met him, she described her own version of my dearest friend to Mom who listened with her mouth opened.

"Francis is probably the murderer and here Patti Rae's been up there…" she motioned toward the woods, "just up there talkin' away with him to beat the band!!" To my relief, Mom tilted her head up to the ceiling giving her entire body over to a good laugh.

"Dear," Mom said, her laughter halting as if on cue. She put the palm of her hand flat on our shiny kitchen table as if needing a solid platform for what she was about to say, "If you're going to be with us for a while you need to know that Patti Rae has quite the imagination. If she could, she'd have us all believing in leprechauns. We all know about her little friend." The discussion ended in more laughter that sounded a bit too delirious to me.

It was plain the morning's events were getting to everybody. So I slipped out the kitchen door, back up into the woods while they checked on the cherry pie that was bubbling out its thick red syrup. I was not even half way to the wood's edge when I heard a loud knock. The sound echoed up to me harshly. I turned to see Jake face to face with Mom. She stood solidly between the opened kitchen door and the door casing.

"You mentioned your car's not runnin' just right the other day," I could barely hear Jake say as he looked around Mom in search of the face that had brought him over. "Thought I'd check it out for ya."

Mom hesitated then looked behind her where Mary Lou sat at our kitchen table.

"Hi Mary Lou," Jake spoke in a soft, hesitant tone. I wondered if Mary Lou's response was as timid. But I wasn't about to go back to find out. The day was too pretty to be penned in by four walls. And the prospect of Mary Lou and Jake? It was just too confusing for me to think about. It was in Mom's hands now, I thought selfishly. I wanted the deep green refuge of my woods even if I couldn't share it with my cousin.

Not less than five trees were so big just beyond the main entrance of the woods that it took six of us kids holding hands to encompass each. One of these trees, that Dad called "virgin timber", was off the main path close by the creek just above my fantasy pool. Its branches lurched out from the creek bank and crept down into the eroding soil below, forming a nice lap for me to sit on. Here I could hide from any kids passing by. I was too tired to look for my dear old Francis after leaving Mary Lou and Mom, so I lay down upon the giant's hand and, as usual, imagined those who'd been here hundreds of years before. Indians.

It was easy. My dad had filled my head with their history and how their ghosts were probably still tied to this land. He loved to talk about how Kentucky used to be a "happy hunting ground" for the Shawnee and other nations. He said our state was so lush and full of game back then, they thought it too sacred to live in. So when white men came along and began to settle, it was cause for death and scalping. So began the raid on pioneers and then wars between the English and French who were able to talk the natives into taking sides. It's what decimated the local Shawnee's tribe. To remedy this decline, they kidnapped pioneer women and children to help re-populate their villages. There were many stories about this strange activity. Most were sad. In Mary Ingle's old age, one of her sons who'd been captured by the Shawnee as a young man, came to visit her years later out of respect. But he was a Shawnee warrior through and through. It broke her heart, Dad said.

I watched these ghosts travel downhill upon our well-worn paths and heard them call to each other. Whippoorwill! Whippoorwill! Tew-wit! Tew-wit! They were everywhere and I watched, immune to their hatchets and their keen sense of sound and smell. From the time I was old enough to learn about these colorful warriors, they became with each passing year, more real with every arrowhead I found beneath a rock or lodged in a stream.

But sometimes they would disappear and the wood nymphs crawled out from one of my favorite books Mom read to me at night. These tiny fairies performed tumbling acts, or bathed themselves in one of the creek pools, or lay supine in a buttercup relaxing in a cool shade. I loved to play with Janey Greene. She was my favorite playmate because she saw all these things too. We chased butterflies, climbed trees, pretended we were Tinker Bell or Peter Pan or Captain Hook. We took turns swinging on our beloved grapevines and fought only about small things.

But sometimes I just liked to be alone in the woods where I could think up new schemes and new games. Then down I'd go in search of Janey to play it out. It wasn't difficult to find her. She was the eldest in a family of eight that included two boys and six girls. Her family was one of the poorest in the neighborhood, and it fell on her to help with house chores relieving her mother of the enormous amount of work it took to rear such a brood. I'd find her stirring something on the stove or hanging out wash on their clothesline. The chores went quickly with two of us working at it and all the while I'd be explaining our game plan. Soon we were in our basement rooting out sheets, old curtains, and Mom's cast-off house dresses.

We painted our faces with Mom's discarded makeup. We used black eyebrow pencil to create faces of lions on our own. With less trouble we became fair maidens. Clothed in just the right garb and painted lips, we took to the woods where all our dreams were played out. Catching lightening bugs was our favorite evening pastime. During the day, we'd lie on our backs in the soft grass and trace a face in a cloud with our finger in the air, trying desperately to get each other to see. When the sun dropped behind our hill, we'd go bicycling down by the railroad yards and take old winding country roads past deserted barns and fields of Queen Anne's Lace. Dangerous forays into a strange wood or the forbidden railroad yards kept our senses keen and our ability to avert danger uncanny. We were wiry, quick, watchful of hobos, but remained dreamy-eyed through it all. We were as well-placed in our world as summer's Tiger Lilies that lurched at us from the road like trumpets.

Someone touched me and I awoke to see two doves looking down at me from a low branch of my giant tree.

"You scared me," I said to Francis whose eyes reflected speckled light escaping high through the trees.

"You better get back down to your company, don't you think?"

"Ahh, she's more interested in talking to Jake right now."

"Well, she likes the woods too. You just scared her."

"How did I scare her?"

"Talking about me. Which is too bad."

"You heard us?" I asked with my face crinkled up.

"I've been keeping a close eye on you. Don't want anything to happen, if you know what I mean?"

"You know, Francis. I can introduce you to Mary Lou. I'd love to…"

"Patti Rae, we've talked about this before. No one's as interested in talking to me as you are. No one wants to meet me."

My desire to bring Francis out of the woods for everyone to see was once again thwarted. I looked at him with a sly smile.

"Don't you want to meet Mary Lou? She's real pretty." His look was far away, a look with which I was unfamiliar. But I pressed on. "She'd like to meet you."

"I don't believe that's true, young lady. I believe your cousin thinks I'm the murderer, does she not?"

I admired my friend's conversational style. Words tumbled out of his mouth as if he were an important person. That's the only way I could express it in those days. I remember the steamy hot afternoon I met him. Some of my friends and I were trudging up the path to the line of hanging grapevines, when I saw him bent over a small bush. Thinking he was an adult from our town on an adult errand—maybe searching for wild berries or looking for Woodland Poppies to transplant—I stopped and watched him place an un-feathered fledgling of a blue bird back into its nest. Without looking at me, he asked if I'd like to see the squawking siblings before the mother returned. I couldn't resist. Their open mouths turned up toward us and their eyes, still closed, looked too big for their tiny skulls. Lovingly, he allowed the branches of the small bush to enclose them once more. Then, stepping into our well-worn path, he introduced himself as Francis.

I said "howdy do". I remarked upon his Catholic name then asked him questions like what was he doing in the woods. He said he owned the woods behind our house and that he was just enjoying them. Where did he live, was my next question. "West", he said and I, having many more questions for this strange man, left "west" alone and went on to other more important questions like, why was he wearing woolen trousers on a summer's day, and why did he let his beard grow so long, and what was his stick for. His laughter shook the woods. I expected my friends to come running but they never did.

I yelled for them, but they were busy swinging from the enduring vines. In the short distance, their laughter filled the woods with summer happiness. But his laugh was different. It didn't resonate naturally but harshly with an inexorable edge of authority. It was an adult laugh.

He told me they were too busy to hear him. So I asked him a few more impertinent questions which he answered with kindness as far as I can re-member. Once he and I seemed satisfied that we had become thoroughly acquainted, he suggested I join my friends again and that I should have a good day. He tipped his pancake-shaped hat and took the path straight up to Hickory Branch Hill Road which made sense to me. His house was up there somewhere, I figured.

"What man?" my friends asked when I rejoined them.

"You didn't see him? You must be blind." I held tight as Janey Greene and I piggy-backed, flying out on an old reliable vine, bringing it down a notch or two. The connecting branches above snapped and cracked, and we screamed at the thought of being deposited onto the tree-tops below. That was the day I met Francis. It seemed so long ago.

Now we were best friends. Francis sat down carefully beside me on the extended tree roots that played host to a soft spreading lichen. A quivering glade enshrined his face.

"Poor, poor lady. What did she ever do to anybody?" Francis turned his tear-filled eyes away from me. Then he spoke clearly, "I highly recommend you not take Mary Lou down to the railroad yards on your bikes while she's here."

Thinking how he was just someone else putting boundaries on my fun, I frowned.

"Did you hear what I said?"

I nodded. Then he also advised me to stay close to my own woods where Mom and everybody were within earshot. He was about to say his usual "good day" when I heard footfalls above us. Turning around quickly, I saw my cousin, Claudia, bouncing down the witch's path. Her mother was my father's beloved sister Aunt Chloe now deceased. Claudia, her father and his second wife—we called her Aunt Bess out of respect—were our neighbors.

"Hey, Patti Rae," she said breathlessly.

"Hey." I said, happy to see a witness. "What were you doin' on the witch path?"

"It's the short cut to the daffodil patch."

"Since when?" I asked.

"Since a long time."

"Why were you at the patch? The flowers are all gone by now."

"Yeah. You're right. Just thought there might be a chance I could get some for the party tonight." I noticed her constant glance over my shoulder.

"Oh," I said. "This is my friend Francis."

She laughed.

"That old crow's name is Francis?"

"Crow?"

I looked behind me. Francis was gone. A black-blue crow had perched itself above me on a high stump. He cocked his narrow head and beak at us then fluttered away in long, graceful sweeps.

"No, Francis is my friend. He was here just a minute ago."

"Sure he was. Patti Rae, you beat all. When you gonna stop making up those outlandish stories?"

"Really, Claudia, he was here just a minute ago!" I turned around to see if I could see him through the thick brush. Perhaps his beret would give him away. But my eyes searched in vain through the jumble of tree trunks and vines. "He's just shy."

"If you say so."

"I do. I mean. No. Really, I think he doesn't like to meet people because what he has to say he only wants the right people to hear. I think it's somethin' like that."

Claudia eyed me cruelly. "So you're the 'right' person?"

"Well, I like it when he talks about how we should all love each other. And he says it like he means it. And I don't laugh at him like some would."

Claudia said decisively, "I'm gonna have to have a talk with your mother."

"Why?"

"'Cause this Francis thing is gettin' out of hand."

I had nothing to say to that.

"You're comin' to my party tonight, arent' ya?" Claudia decided wisely to change the subject.

"Nobody told me you were havin' a party. What kinda party?"

"My birthday party! Didn't Bob tell you and Mary Lou?"

Immediately, I wondered if Mary Lou had been told and I, as usual, had been left out.

"He probably told Mary Lou but not me."

"Hey, don't worry about that. I've invited you and that's that." Claudia sharply nodded her head with each 'that' and I wondered what was up.

"And do me a favor. Don't forget to tell Mary Lou Chad's gonna to be there. He asked me to tell you to make sure she knows he'll be there." Claudia took my arm to make this point.

"Well, why don't he call her and tell her himself?"

"He's afraid to," was her answer.

I rolled my eyes.

So she added, "Bess says everybody's afraid right now 'cause of the murder and it's best he don't call her. Oh my gosh! Can you believe someone got murdered that close to us?"

"What's this have to do with…."

Claudia interrupted me. "Sides, he's afraid of party lines. His mom's best friend is on yours."

I couldn't believe my ears. There's no way in the whole wide world that Chad could have been the murderer. And who cared if somebody listened in on their party line? It was the rule and not the exception. Mom had informed me once, in one of her sterner moments, that not having secrets was a good thing. And I, not having any at that moment, wholeheartedly agreed. I looked down into our valley, the road and houses appearing like footnotes through the trees. I can't remember why, but I was a bit thrown off. It seemed a subtle change in the landscape had taken place. It was as if I were looking at something familiar for the first time from a different vantage point. But oddly, it was from the same vantage point. It was the first of many metaphysical geographical mysteries I would have throughout my life. Dad said it was natural to have things like that happen. To him, it was just a simple matter of growing pains.

"Oh, and don't forget to tell Francis 'hi' for me the next time you see him," Claudia yelled back at me as she continued her jaunty descent following the main path.

I smiled because I knew, somewhere, he was watching.

CHAPTER 8

Agony & Ecstasy

Lots of colorful balloons. Loud music. Dancing. Finding romance in a coal bin or behind a furnace. A 1950's party.

For the middle-American teenager during this period, most parties were thrown in dark and foreboding basements. The era of full entitlement for adolescents had yet to come into its own. But teenagers didn't seem to mind. That someone had been given the permission to have a party was the only thing that mattered. Claudia's birthday party was no different. Everyone wanted to come.

I remember helping her blow up the balloons. There were so many, we ran out of floor joists to hang them on. We also tacked up sweeping crepe paper which somehow caught a more sophisticated mood and conjured up a feeling of brighter places like the extravagant Lookout House on Dixie Highway we'd all seen pictures of. And I'll never forget Uncle Roland's new but slightly dented Coca Cola cooler. Its red body beamed up at us as we entered Claudia's party den. Inside, spaced closely together in a nest of chipped ice, were stocked soft drinks of all brands and colors. At three o'clock that afternoon, Uncle Roland had lugged the heavy metal cooler downstairs. Inside its aluminum walls he propped up the bottles. Sitting on the edge of a wooden office chair, he hammered away at a large block of ice with confident swings using a dangerous-looking ice pick. Each sliver and gravel fallen from grace was placed carefully around the thick-glassed bottles in what seemed the most artful preparation of the day. My father had accompanied Uncle Roland to the ice house earlier that afternoon. They'd used his military blanket in which to nest the formidable cube of glass. It went without saying. All parties required a trip to the ice house.

Through the opened garage door, chirring of cicadas pushed through the late afternoon air as Mary Lou and I considered the offerings inside Uncle Roland's cooler: Barq's rootbeer, cream soda, Coca Cola, 7-Up. I lifted a bottle from the venerable box and gulped down my first red soda of the night. Two or three bottles had already been grabbed by some of Claudia's closest friends who had arrived already. Over by the wringer washing machine, they practiced a new jitterbug move, the convolutions of which involved looping of arms around necks, then a foot crawl away from each other.

Earlier, Mary Lou and I trudged down to Claudia's house to help with the posters. We worked feverishly so none of us would miss The Mouseketeers and Superman, television programs that began airing at four o'clock in the afternoon. Claudia hooked up the record player next to the water pump. When Uncle Roland found out, he marched up to her, his face tense.

"You got lots of space to put it over there," he yelled pointing to a dryer section of the basement closer to the garage door.

"But Dad," Claudia argued. "That's gonna be in our way when we dance!"

We covered the furnace with posters that said things like "Happy Birthday Sweet Sixteen" and "Rock Around the Furnace Tonight" with Bill Haley and the Comet's picture pasted on one side. The crepe paper streams eventually stretched and hung low from their thumbtack points, hitting our heads gently as we walked beneath them. Claudia placed a balloon on all four corners of the cake table.

"Well, now. Isn't that smart," Mary Lou's lengthened vowels ribboned out into the commotion like satin. Claudia and I stopped to listen but said nothing. We'd been warned by our parents not to talk about Mary Lou's accent. The reason for that had never been explained to me. I went along with it even though there were times I felt her voice transported me to a place of secure beauty. If I could have explained it like that in so many words back then, I would have told her.

Upstairs, zigzags of white icing fell unevenly around the sides of Claudia's birthday cake. But Aunt Bess, mouth pursed and beads of sweat appearing on her upper lip, forged ahead seeming blissfully unaware of her mistakes. The pink candles and hard-sugar flowers pushed into the top of the cake made her unsteady handiwork around the sides less noticeable. I brought this to her attention and was surprised at the unappreciative response.

Around 6:30 p.m. Claudia turned up the volume on her record player as an army of teenagers charged down the hill to her house. Some had been dropped off by parents. Others, old enough, drove themselves. Sync, a thick-bodied senior who attended Catholic school in town, floated dramatically down the asphalt drive in his white convertible. Elvis's "Hound Dog" cried out from his dash. The raging crescendos echoed up the street, alerting anyone within a mile that teenagers were gathering somewhere in our small town.

"Isn't he a living doll?" My cousin's best friend, Judy, asked this unnecessary question. Judy stood up straight, smoothing her skirt, expecting he might look at her any second. Some yelled "hello" to Sync from inside where his name bounced off the concrete walls. His dramatic entrance was a success. As if his good looks weren't enough, Sync hurled his body and muscular legs over the driver's door instead of opening it. Wearing pegged blue jeans, brushed white bucks and a "Detroit" hairstyle – short on top, long and brushed back on the sides – he was the epitome of "cool." Even the guys idolized him. Bob called him a "cool cat" one night at the supper table without thinking. Dad ordered Bob to leave the table with the stipulation he could re-join us once his language had gained respectability. "And whoever heard of such a name?" Dad's voice trailed Bob upstairs to his bedroom.

The remainder of the evening, Sync's red-interior convertible sat like a gaudy ornament just outside the garage door that yawned music into the tremulous night air. To Mary Lou, I gave a run-down of Sync's many wonderful attributes. I observed her closely to gauge the reaction. But it was easy to see. He didn't thrill her. It occurred to me that maybe he was too big for her—in the dramatic sense that is. That maybe the stage she usually dominated was not big enough for both egos. In terms of their appearance, though, they were a perfect fit.

Mary Lou slumped to indicate boredom after my barrage of Sync information. She'd just crunched into a potato chip, eyes half-closed, when someone of more interest slid inside the door. Jake wasn't so tall as he was a thin, human board of plywood. My cousin whose thick hair, now haloed from the humidity, voluptuous and suddenly alive, left my company to stand next to Jake's slip of a body. As they communicated, heads close and eyes locked, I watched in horror. What if Aunt Bess came downstairs and caught her niece sidled up to Jake? The beautiful and stunning Mary Lou with Jake! Jake dressed in black... Jake who represented everything for which Aunt Bess had a distinct disdain. With short breaths, as I watched their communion of obvious passion, my thoughts turned to Claudia. Poor Aunt Bess. Little did she know her own stepdaughter had a crush on Jake that was going on two years. But Aunt Bess stayed upstairs. For now, we'd averted any natural catastrophes.

The warm night played out in dances, popped balloons and general squealing. Trite confessions...that so and so was in love with so and so... geared emotions up like an over-wound clock.

"But he doesn't even know I exist," a girl in pink pedal pushers moaned. Hoping that Sync might catch her words through a confusion of noise, she swooned in his direction. This was followed by giggles rippling through layers of music. But the words imperfectly reached his ears. Sync was lost in his own masculine world of put-downs, shoving and shouting...the male form of flirtation that canceled out the girls'.

Then there was Jake. It was hard not to feel sorry for him. He stood in the corner with Mary Lou who glanced over her shoulder from time to time in her coy manner. Was she enticing someone else with her fluttering eyelashes? I couldn't tell. I hoped not. My thoughts ran in Jake's favor as I considered what a really nice person he was despite his social disadvantages. Just that past winter, three weeks before Christmas, he had helped me with my fractions one night when he was supposed to be visiting Bob. I remember how he patted my head whenever I got a problem right. The other boys upstairs were making a racket, throwing marbles down our hardwood stairs. They were laughing, yelling and generally getting yelled at by my father. Jake hadn't seemed to be missing anything. I remember how he looked around and smiled at Mom whenever she waltzed by the kitchen table where my homework spread out in an unhappy disarray. Like the other boys, he called my mother 'Mrs. John-son' and was good at the 'yes ma'am', 'no ma'am' thing. Maybe better than the rest. But to criticize him for that would have been unfair. He seemed to understand his situation better than we did. We never told him we weren't allowed to go over to his house but he surely must have guessed.

I drifted over to their corner.

"Jake, why dontcha ask Mary Lou to dance?"

He self-consciously looked out into the sea of slow dancers. Guys were gripping girls around their cinched waists, edging beyond the bounds of ac-cepted public behavior. To increase the excitement, Claudia had flipped off the lights, leaving only the soft glow of lamps in a small adjoining basement room that overlooked the back yard.

Mary Lou twined her delicate fingers around Jake's worn hand. With a little tug and some backward prancing, she pulled him out of the dark cor-ner and onto the dance floor. Up to this point, Claudia hadn't even realized Jake was there. It was the sight of them in the dimness that brought her to a standstill, as if someone had just told her she had only ten days to live. She hadn't invited Jake to the party, I later learned. I watched as she visibly shook off the surprise. She marched toward them with some futile purpose, then stopped again. Their complete infatuation was unmistakable. It was no use. She turned and detoured upstairs as if to tend to something urgently pressing. Publicly she would never say she was sweet on Jake, but her jealous looks their way told everyone what we already knew.

"Okay! Enough of that!" Claudia called out once back down the stairs. It was a general statement, but everybody looked at Jake and Mary Lou who were still oblivious to everyone but each other.

Rosy-cheeked and in a summer sweat that tightened blond curls into ringlets, Claudia threw herself into the next fast dance after bringing up the lights. She had everyone's complete attention now. After all, it was her party, her birthday. Twirling, rocking, rolling, we watched amused to see her in overdrive. Without much effort, Bobby Lee swung her under his legs, her crinolines flaring to reveal her cotton underwear. Claudia had effectively ended the romantic siege of "Are You Lonesome Tonight."

From then on, she kept a keen eye on Mary Lou and Jake. I walked over and sat next to Chad who was also not happy to see Mary Lou so romantically involved. He put his arm around me and asked how I liked my new houseguest. I said I liked her a lot. I could see from his forlorn face, he did too.

"Well, Chad. There's no reason why you can't ask her for the next dance. She won't say 'no'...I don't think."

But she did say "no" simply because she didn't know how to jitterbug. So they talked about his uncle's car and Chad's position on his high school's football team. By taking her arm sometimes to make a point, he was pulling her slowly away from Jake and into his own corner where two chairs sat conveniently open. Chad's fascination with Mary Lou's accent was initially civil. But with growing confidence, he became impulsive. In horror, I listened as he impersonated her lengthened vowels. She only laughed. Then he told her how beautiful he thought she was. Would she send him her next class picture through the mail? He'd be sure to give her his address later.

On the other side of the room, time slowed to an agonizing dirge. Jake stood alone in the corner scrutinizing the complex rhythms of adolescence. One-two-cha-cha-cha. Buddy and a small girl in a blue tight skirt caught Jake's attention, and he watched like a student who would soon take to the dance floor. But I suspected it was his only way to participate...to seem not too obviously removed from a world he wished he were part of. It was about this time that we heard a scream from the driveway.

"It's the murderer! Oh God! It's the man who killed her!"

It was Judy. Her eyes were glued to something on the hill from across the creek. The entire party gushed out of the garage door to stand by her side.

"Where?!"

"There!" She pointed her shaking finger.

We spotted the tall figure right away. It lumbered down the hill toward Aunt Bess's house. In its hand was a gun and a purposefulness in its gait that was fearful.

A rush of bodies tumbled back inside the garage door upsetting the fold-up table that held four stacks of forty-fives. The black vinyl discs rolled and slid across the concrete floor creating their own little stampede. Some were trampled on. Some cracked in two.

"Put the door down!"

My brother and Chad strained to bring it down but it was locked at some unknown point.

"Get out of the way!" Claudia yelled then, hands shaking, unhooked something above that brought the wooden garage door slamming to the floor. With a quaking noise and a horrible vibration to the house, it jolted my mind into a dark place where life suddenly offered itself up like fragile china. It was as if the usual safety nets had disappeared into a dungeon that seemed a perfect trap. We were in a tomb! Loud screams shrilly bouncing off close concrete walls was the sound of death. I had to remind myself to breathe. The clinging of girls to girls and girls to boys turned a picture of passion into terror. It was a morbid reminder of the woman's death and of our own mortality as much as I could grasp what that meant. The panic may have lasted only thirty, forty seconds but it seemed a lifetime of fear.

In this sea of terror, there was only one person who appeared calm and unwilling to relent to an encroaching evil. Jake.

"Hold on just a minute," he said reflexively. I thought he turned toward the back room door to make sure it was locked. But with as much surprise as anyone, I watched his slender figure open the door and step out into full view of the killer. We heard him calling to Gilbert.

"You better put that gun away!" He said laughing loud enough so that we could hear. "You've scared 'em half ta death."

Then Jake's voice trailed off and we picked up a faint mention of squirrel hunting as we peered out the back windows. He and Gilbert were laughing together now. The sound of their voices seemed at ease and disrespectful of the solid fear inside. It made Jake seem much older than us and I wondered if anyone else felt humiliated like I did.

Gilbert and Jake strolled over to the driveway and stood in front of the closed garage door. They held each other's attention like old hunting buddies except that I could see through the garage door windows that something inexplicably grave was between them. But for Claudia, it was time to put the pieces of the party back together. She lifted the garage door with a "shiiii" in their direction. When the music flared up again, it didn't seem to suit Gilbert. Agitated, I heard him say "...so better watch your step, son." Jake nodded his head with surprising compliance. Poor Jake, I thought. It seemed he was always watching his step. Gilbert directed a few more serious words his way. They shook hands. Then the old squirrel hunter ambled back down the hill toward the creek shouldering his shotgun. Music once again pumped its rhythms out into the quickening twilight. I watched Jake who seemed even more removed from the fun than before. His face had suddenly turned white. It seemed he wanted to go but wanted to stay at the same time.

Claudia took care of that. She brushed off the last toppled forty-five then placed it on top of a thick pile of vinyl disks waiting patiently to be dropped to the turn-table. Then, after looking upstairs and a general glance around, she flew outside to Jake's side and led him away from the garage door. I left the back way and made a circuit around the house so I could spy on them. Hoping no one would see me, I crawled behind Aunt Bess's shrubs close by where they stood.

"Bess'd be mad if she knew you were here, ya know," Claudia told Jake in the coldest terms.

"I've been standing near the door just in case she came down," he admitted.

"Well what if she came around from the front and walked in and there you are, big as you please, with little Miss Mary Lou... and you starin' at her like a stag in heat!"

"Don't talk like that Claudia. It's not lady-like."

"Oh! So I guess Mary Lou wouldn't say nothin' like that, now would she?"

Jake looked blankly into Claudia's eyes. I could see the importance he'd attached to her in the past had now diminished considerably.

"At least get rid of them fags! You know how Bess feels about those nasty ole things. She can be such an ass."

Jake looked down at the cigarettes as if considering their importance.

"You know, you really should call Bess 'Mom'. After all she treats you like you were her very own."

"She don't care much about me, really." Claudia looked down. "She just does lots for me to make Dad happy."

"She loves you Claudia. And, when it comes to me…she's just being protective."

"Well if you like her so much, why dontcha give up those nasty cigarettes. She thinks they're disgusting!" Claudia sneered at his right bicep where a rolled sleeve embraced a pack of Camels.

With a blunt flip, Jake hurled them behind the bush that hid me from view. Glancing off my head with a soft thud, they fell to the damp ground where June bugs and Grandaddy Long Legs tried out the shiny red and white surface. I flicked them off and brought Jake's favorite Camels to my nose. I breathed in their sweet tobacco smell.

"Go down to the creek and I'll meet you in about an hour. By then Bess'll have brought down the birthday cake and I'll bring some to you." She turned her face up for a kiss.

Jake stepped back from her lips probably for the first time, I thought. But it didn't hold Claudia back. She pecked brusquely at his undefended cheek. Before retreating back into the noise and fun of the party, she threatened me.

"Patti Rae, if you smoke those cigarettes, I'm gonna tell your mom."

I didn't say a word just in case she was guessing.

When Jake bent wearily over to retrieve his smokes, I handed them to him through the bushes. He wheezed a dry laugh. I came out from behind the shrubs brushing myself, giggling and hoping he'd notice the poodle skirt Mom had made for me that very afternoon. But there were no compliments. It was clear that whatever words he might have at that point were burned black. They would have caught in his throat. And his eyes said it all. I wanted to reassure him but he turned and slipped down to the creek just as Claudia had suggested. Blue cigarette smoke trailed behind him, a melancholy streamer of existence that floated on the night air giving up its tobacco aroma little by little.

As I stood looking down at Jake, I saw flashes of his arm throwing small rocks into the rippling depths. Behind me, I heard the noise of tire treads feeling their way down the drive. A long, red convertible with pink dice dangling from its rearview mirror, sidled up next to Sync's car by the open garage door. A petite brunette sitting above the back seat, almost on the trunk, dangled her legs between two boys who held tight to her ankles. Her white angora sweater spread tightly across ample breasts and looked hot in the eighty degree temperature. She and her two friends disappeared into the basement without saying 'hey' so I followed on their heels being as invisible to them as the owners of the house they entered. It seemed the brunette had her sights on Chad all along. She dragged him onto the dance floor without saying hello to a soul. Mary Lou watched them self-consciously. But it was Claudia who demanded attention on the dance floor more than anyone. In this familiar element, Claudia had eclipsed Mary Lou. It was obvious Mary Lou felt the shadow keenly as she watched her cousin bounce from one boy to the next. I think she decided to pretend she wasn't watching by coming up to me at the cake table.

"Where'd Jake go?"

"Claudia told him he isn't welcome. So he's down by the creek."

Mary Lou stiffened.

"Why did she…"

Angry, and with a puff of exasperation, she wiped potato chip grease off her fragile finger tips, flung a napkin to the floor and swirled around to go find him. In a flash, I pulled off my top crinoline. Down by the creek they would be able to hear its rustle.

Jake had chosen a large sycamore on which to lean his thin back. Mary Lou angled next to him on the ground with her skirt spread out like a cloud. Their heads seemed so close, I thought they must be touching or kissing. I could see I needed to make a wide circle to stay out of their sight as a long shadow preceded me from the outside light. Aunt Bess had decided the flood light was necessary now that dusk was falling. Soon I was behind the tree and could hear everything perfectly.

"You can come to any of my parties at home. Any time. You're better than the rest of 'em, really. I hate my cousin for being this way," Mary Lou pouted.

"Don't say things like that about your family. Family's the most important thing we got, ya know."

"Yeah?"

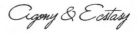

"Yeah. Everybody thinks my Dad's nothin' but a no good drunk and mostly he is, but he's still my Dad and I know he loves me." He pulled tall weeds growing by the trunk of the tree, fidgeting and revealing inner turmoil. "There was a time when me, Mom and my sisters was everything to him."

"That's nice," Mary Lou cooed.

"Now he has to be everything to us or we'd lose him for sure. There's not a night goes by but we don't go lookin' for him."

I could see their cross-starred images in the calm of the creek and watched Mary Lou's reflection plant a soft kiss on Jake's cheek. He only turned to her and took her hand. There was no lunging, no urgent pressing upon her. It was as if restraint was an unwritten law for him. But his reticence fueled Mary Lou's inner-most engines. She began to breathe so heavily, I could hear its impatient rushing through the warm night air.

"I'll always love you like this," she spooled her extra vowels into his ear. "What I mean is that no matter what happens, this starry night, the tree frogs, the cicadas, your handsome face lookin' down at me and this here creek rippling right next to us. Your soft touch…" Then she took his other hand and placed it on her chest indicating her heart. "They will always be here."

Jake brought his hand back to his side but leaned over to take the kiss that had been promised from the very first. He kissed Mary Lou's lips as if they were rose petals, as if they would fall to the ground if pressed too hard.

I could feel it rising quickly in my throat. Two bottles of crème soda downed greedily now threatened to come up on me. So I went down the creek to the small rock dam and crossed over to the other side. Here I could watch without being heard or seen. The field grass was full of chiggers I suspected. So I pounded the tall growth down. After deftly making an indention by dragging my feet in a circle, I noticed a dark figure walking slowly toward me in the distance. I stopped suddenly, holding my breath. But it was only Francis. Relaxing, I belched within his earshot.

"You shouldn't spy on lovers," Francis whispered squatting down close to me while he chewed on a strand of rye grass.

"If you don't think so, then why are you here?"

"Been over to the railroad yards. Thought I'd take a look around to see if I could find something out about the murderer."

"Well didja?"

"Not a thing," Francis spat out the last word with the juice he'd conjured up in his mouth. "I feel sorry for your cousin, you know."

"Why's that?"

"She's quite different. Maybe even wise for her age. Anyway, she understands the hurt to Jake's pride."

"How do you know his pride's been hurt?"

"I can see it. Can't you?"

I nodded my head. "I just know it has been hurt. He knows he's not welcome up there." I indicated Aunt Bess' house with my eyes.

"It's all right. He'll be okay in the long run. And she will too. But for now, their being together is only going to create difficulties." Francis scratched his head. "Why don't you try to get her interested in Chad. You think that would work?"

"No."

Francis laughed.

"Hey, how do you know Chad's interested?" I asked in a high pitch that brought Jake and Mary Lou's heads up momentarily.

"Shhhh," Francis warned. Then he lifted one shoulder.

"He is for a fact but how'd you know that?"

Francis drew closer so they wouldn't hear us again. "You're right," he said finally. "I guess these things have to be worked out on their own. After all, only we know who we can love."

My dear old wise friend helped me to my feet and made sure I didn't stumble into the creek as we balanced our way across the narrow, sharp-edged rock dam. The moonlight behind us cast Francis' shadow in the trebling creek, a shadow that seemed as alive as the minnows that swam in its shallows during the day. I wondered how it was Peter Pan ever lost his shadow and if he felt as badly losing it as I would have losing Francis'. We left Mary Lou and Jake that night under the sycamore tree and the stars that clamored in the sky as they bumped against each other. It was a sky that warned. But I'll always remember it as one of the brightest and most beautiful.

Francis crossed the road as I said goodbye. Inside, the basement seemed to have shrunken in size with each new guest. The salty smell of perspiration lay heavy in the dank air. The small phonograph volleyed its clanging music into a loose tapestry of shrill conversations. After the lilting sounds of a full-mooned night, it was an affront to my ears.

But the night was far from over. They came just as I'd tapped Chad's shoulder to see if he'd dance with me. Two policemen in a cruiser tore down Aunt Bess's drive with lights flashing. We heard a hard knocking at the front door upstairs. Claudia bolted over to the record player to cut off the music. The officers' footfalls were followed by every upward-looking eye in the basement. Then, slowly, they clopped their way down the stairs into the now quiet humanity that had been a party. They looked around sternly, said something to Aunt Bess, then left.

"What happened, Bess? Who are they lookin' for?" Claudia whined.

"Oh it's nothing, Sweetheart. They just had the wrong house. You all go on and have a good time. I'll bring the cake down in a few minutes."

I imagined Claudia made a note to take a piece to her abused Jake. But Jake was with Mary Lou now. They were saying their goodbyes standing just outside, next to the cars in the drive. Mary Lou went upstairs to say goodnight to Aunt Bess and Uncle Roland while Jake lingered a moment longer basking in the night as if it were his last experience outside an imagined prison. The newly arrived red convertible caught his attention briefly when its owner and the owner's buddy shuffled out to smoke.

"Hey!" The tall football player in the letter sweater yelled crossly. "What's the big idea?"

"Just admiring your wheels," Jake said.

Both young men eyed Jake suspiciously.

"What's a hood like you doin' at a party like this anyhow?"

I could see Jake's first impulse was to punch. But his tight fists relaxed almost immediately. Perhaps he remembered his last scuffle with another jock that Bob had told us about. There was a long brawl and the jock had won.

"Couldn't say," Jake mumbled to himself as he walked away, muscles tense, cautiously anticipating a surprise attack. But no one came after him. From behind Sync's car that sparkled white and shimmered under the floodlight, I watched Jake walk up the drive and disappear into the darkness.

The party that was not recorded in the local paper, that may now be unrecorded in Claudia's memories, resumed. But I remember the questions, the wild rumors about who the murderer could be that filled the basement of that small white cottage in our small country town. Mostly I remember the forty-five tunes blaring out of an inadequate green speaker box. Their modern rhythms led the party back into its chaotic exuberance of dance, its new socially unacceptable behavior and teenage embarrassments.

CHAPTER 9

The Give-Away

Mom wasn't in a good mood. Then she had to walk by the kitchen screen door at the wrong time. Bob's friends had just come up from the road and had positioned themselves just outside the door so she wouldn't see them. But now she had, and she was aggravated. She knew why they stood in a little clump, shoulders bowed. They were waiting for a glimpse of Mary Lou. Their faces were serious and long with the anxious look of taxed predators.

"Boys, g'won and get away from the door!"

Mom's shrill command jolted them. All three jumped straight up into the air like green frogs in a puddle. But it took more than Mom's threat to break their resolve. Without turning and still watching for a glimpse of Mary Lou, they edged away from our kitchen door by taking only two steps back.

Inside, Bob had made a mess. It wasn't often mom yelled at his friends. Seeing them jump all at the same time, my brother had spewed orange juice from his full mouth. Then began his uncontrollable laugh which appeared to be set on a crash course. I cringed then giggled as I watched this unfolding drama. Mom told me to eat my eggs, then gave Bob a searing look which cut his hysteria short. He didn't have to be told to clean up the table. But it did seem almost too daunting a task for his adolescent brain. Where would he start? The paper towels didn't appear to be an obvious option nor did the dish clothe lying wet on the sink. For a minute, I thought he was going to run for the mop. Finally, he settled on the cleanest hand towel he could find from a pile of folded linen. With it he soaked up the rejected juice that, by then, had formed tributaries leading off the edge of our table. Mary Lou, for the first time that morning, seemed to be aware of what was going on. She ducked her head and grinned down at her breakfast.

It was more than Mom could take. She turned toward the door again.

"Go home or on down to the park and play baseball or somethin' so we can finish our breakfast in peace!"

She obviously hadn't slept well and everyone was on edge. Everyone but Mary Lou. A glowing smile, seeming to emanate from some unknown source, held us all at a confused distance. Eventually, Mom's anger passed into something else:

"So what's your Momma doin' with herself these days?"

Mary Lou continued daydreaming not realizing she'd been addressed. So Mom forged ahead, her head lurching forward a bit. "She still quiltin'? Your Dad still playin' the fiddle?" Mary Lou stirred to the barest attention, only slightly minding good manners, then sat upright.

"Dad's still sawin' on that old fiddle. Yes ma'am. And Mom...she doesn't do much quiltin' anymore 'cause of arthritis." Mary Lou spoke politely between bites. "She keeps sayin' she's gonna teach me but I'm always busy with school and my pets."

Mom cast a look of disapproval Mary Lou's way. Mary Lou noticed.

"You know, feedin' em and keepin' fresh straw 'n everything in the barn." In her own defense that I was glad she took, Mary Lou added, "And I milk the cows for Dad sometimes, too. And I keep Freckles curried and walked."

"You keep yourself prettily combed yourself."

Mary Lou and I forced pathetic laughs in order, I think, to confirm that Mom's remark was innocent and without sarcasm.

Mom got up two or three times, looked out the window to keep an eye on the boys, probably wishing she hadn't yelled at them. She wiped her red hands on the full white embroidered apron which she tied in two places every morning. Behind her neck and around her waist. Her apron pockets were usually filled with tools that would help her through the day...handkerchiefs, rubber bands, safety pins, clothespins and Mercurochrome. One day she dipped her hand into one of the apron pockets and found a sleeve section of a sewing pattern that she thought had been lost. She celebrated her find the rest of the day. Mom's apron wasn't just a part of her. It was her. She edged back to the table.

"Bob's growin' up. Tall as his dad." It was a wistful attempt to get a compliment from Mary Lou. 'Yes, he's quite handsome' would have been nice, but Mary Lou continued her inscrutable smile and nodded.

We were gathering up the dishes when Dad made his fresh-shaven morning entrance.

"Good mornin' everyone."

Only Mary Lou returned his greeting. The high tenor in Dad's usual mumbling morning voice elicited a surprised look from both Mom and me. Despite his overly formal voice, however, Mom was kind, faintly restraining a smile.

"So you and Gilbert are getting up a meeting tonight?" Mom inquired and confirmed at the same time.

"Yep. It's not going to be pretty."

Mom directed her gaze from Dad to us with only a slightly disguised concern.

"I don't mind letting them know, Martha. They're big girls."

We trained our eyes on my father, ready for anything…good news, bad news. I was always eager to hear something different. And if it turned out to be bad news, even shocking, my world usually never changed that much. My parents were barrier reefs protecting my childhood shores.

"We think we know who murdered that woman the other night so the town council's meeting this evening to do something about it." I noticed a hesitancy in Dad's voice that occurred sometimes when his thoughts moved in opposing directions.

"Of course, these things are never good." He was in command again. "Can sometimes turn bad. But we're pretty sure we've got evidence."

I was wild with curiosity.

"Who do you think done it, Dad?"

"Did it, Patti Rae."

"Who do you think did it?"

"I don't want to say yet, but don't worry. We've got our eye on him so he won't be goin' anywhere without the Sheriff on his trail. But just in case, you two probably better stay in today."

"But who is it, Dad?"

"Too soon to tell and too soon for accusations."

"But Dad! Do we know him?!"

"Patti Rae, eat your cereal and hush!"

Mom's threatening looks and commands had not done the job, but the pattering rain, which had been ushered in by humid warm wind, dispersed the crowd of unlucky boys.

The day proceeded full of gloom, foreboding, and rain. It was usually during such periods of grayness that I turned to my books for entertainment. On this day, however, they held no allure. Mary Lou played Chinese Checkers with Bob, and I could hear their laughter all the way upstairs. I came down to join in the fun, but Bob said I wasn't wanted. Mary Lou kept silent. So I went back upstairs again and, somewhere in the middle of a Nancy Drew mystery, fell asleep. I awoke only to hear Mom's complaints about the heat. She had remained in a bad mood, and her flinty sighs of distress traveled up the staircase and trailed past my ears like an argument. It seemed the oven and pressure cooker were giving off more heat than she could bear. So she slammed the kitchen door, escaping to her garden, I supposed. For a few minutes, I wondered at her strength and how it was she could cook so many meals day after day with so few breaks.

Suddenly a golden shimmer of light filtered through my window like an unexpected song. The grass below glowed in iridescent yellow and spring green. Small puffs of cooler after-rain air danced into my room and, at once, my mood lifted. It was five o'clock.

"Everybody, come on in for supper!"

Mom's voice was high and melodious, transformed suddenly by the surprise visit of sunlight and cool breezes through our kitchen boathouse windows. The pale yellow beams of late sun travelled across our table as we gathered for our last meal of the day. They spotlighted suspended dust particles – a reminder we breathed more than air. We watched their floating dances while eating without comment. When cherry cobbler was served up for dessert, a shiny new topic of conversation was spawned: Mom's superb cooking. Then Dad told a joke and fell into his old habit of reminiscing. His voice resonated handsomely in my ear and seemed somehow related to the sudden change in temperature. Something kind from nature. And there was that look of affection that fell from Mom's face onto Dad's as if all she ever really wanted was to make him happy. Looking back, I realize Mom's Swiss steak, mashed potatoes and cherry cobbler were mere backdrops for the welcome breeze and light swathing us in surreal gold. Every detail of that family meal is now a jeweled trinket locked up in the safe of my mind.

That night Bob's friends came over again, only this time they were invited. Jake wasn't. I was relieved to hear it. I had been worrying about Mary Lou's infatuation with him and how their flirtations might set off alarms in our house.

After the orange juice debacle, Bob had intelligently offered to do the dishes. Then, to my surprise, he asked Mom if he could have his own little party that night. Even more to my surprise, she agreed. If Mom could have foreseen Mary Lou would be the only girl in attendance, I don't think the party would have happened. It wasn't that Bob hadn't invited other girls. It was just that none showed up.

At six o'clock, an all-male crowd of teenagers met in our living room. The jumpy assembly wasn't without its shoving and pushing and the usual hitting of heads. But then Mary Lou made her entry, casting nervous silence over the party. I can still recall each of their anxious expressions. In the close sultry air, all of us sat a bit stiffly listening to Elvis and Chuck Berry as their tunes hissed out from our little wooden box radio sitting in the corner. Attached to the top of this revered box was a shiny black handle for carrying. Only one white circle graced its front. Inside this glass face at center was a thin, black dial that rotated by turning a corresponding knob for the purpose of searching out stations. Bob's five buddies weren't happy with the current music so he adjusted the dial while they sat straight-backed watching every twitch and swoop of Mary Lou's theatrics. All of us, especially Chad, sweat through our clothes even with all the windows open. No one had struck up conversation, and it served as an agonizing reminder to Bob's friends that they were yet unable to successfully communicate with a girl. To fill in the excruciating social gaps, feet tapped nervously, knees bounced, sometimes keeping time to the music. Often, in tragic desperation, the same knees went into a vibrating frenzy. Sounds of cracked knuckles contrasted the measured bump and whirr of our little green fan that alternated from right to left, then left to right. At the center of this nervous energy, Mary Lou appeared dry and cool, oblivious to the eighty-nine degree temperature. This had something to do, I surmised, with the perfumed handkerchief she used to pat her face and neck. I'd seen her use a handkerchief in recent days to great effect. But tonight she flapped and fluttered it around her face so much it had us all hypnotized. We'd never seen anyone afraid to sweat.

Lurching like an unwelcome adult upon the scene, a news break destroyed what the guys, no doubt, perceived as a hip atmosphere.

"Today President Eisenhower..."

Bob quickly turned the small knob again, whisking us out of grown-up reality in search of what little rock 'n roll magic floated in those fifties airwaves.

"Lordy," Mary Lou said, blowing her bangs up from her forehead. "When's the rest of the party comin'?"

Her impatience reminded me of a thoroughbred's lust for racing and never hearing the bell enough times during the day.

Wanting to appear as feminine as my cousin, I left to retrieve a lace hand-kerchief out of Mom's vanity drawer. I doused it with some of her Muguet de Bois cologne and tried to keep up the pace. No one noticed my antics, however, except Bobby Lee who said I was doing it all wrong. So I gave up. When I left the room to put the unsuccessful lace back in its drawer, I noticed more conversation, some giggling and a general perking up in my absence. Understanding that maybe I had created some tension, that perhaps they perceived me as the eyes and ears of parents, I chose to remain in the next room, watching furtively through a crack in the door.

I was surprised that it was Bob who finally got up enough nerve to ask Mary Lou to dance. To his horror, she didn't know how to jitterbug.

"You don't know how to jitterbug?!"

"No."

"You don't know how to jitterbug?!" Bob repeated in a louder voice.

"I said I didn't!"

So Bob gave her a basic lesson in the art form.

Pretending to admire Bob's rocking and rolling moves that were pure comedy, she followed as best she could, filling in the missing parts. The guys were relieved to have something to laugh about. Once Mary Lou held her fingers to her smiling lips, but Bob was too busy clogging the carpet to notice.

Now warmed up and confident of his rhythm, Bob took Mary Lou's hands and without much effort, she found the beat. It was interesting to see how quickly she learned. It was as if she understood the music intrinsically and how it dictated her moves. Bass sound, dip, up between the half beats.

"Where'd you learn to dance like that?" she asked but Bob only smiled, taking it as a compliment rather than a question. He didn't think to comment on her superior natural ability.

After a while, I recognized their individual rhythms had finally come together in some vague form of a jitterbug. It seemed they inhabited a cosmos of their own as they pumped their legs and spirits high into the atmosphere, unlike the low spirits waxing edgy in the corners of our living room. The guys were angry because Bob was dancing with the princess and having all the fun, the unfairness of this being that Bob was her cousin. So when a slow tune slipped in, Chad tapped Bob's shoulder with maybe a bit too much pressure. He took Mary Lou's hands tentatively then slowly wrapped one arm half-way around her waist. Their weaving shoulders made me dizzy.

"It's a bad situation in there," I told Mom who sat outside in near darkness on the back patio snapping beans for next day's supper. "All them jittery boys in a sweat and just one girl."

"Lordy," Mom breathed out.

"You been out here for a long time pickin' beans, haven't you?" I said placing myself next to Mom and stringing a few beans, imagining that I was help to her.

"Yes, I have and my back's killin' me."

"Then why dontcha sit on Dad's big chair instead of sittin' on these old concrete steps?"

"I like the view from here," she said, indicating that perhaps there was some way to derive satisfaction from house work.

I looked at the stairs that ran down from our patio, becoming a sidewalk running a straight line along the side of our house. It took a left turn at our front porch and then fell twelve steps more, leading to the lower plateau of our yard. Here it, once again, turned left commencing into two steps leading further onto our driveway. From the driveway, one had to walk a few more paces to reach the county road. Ours was a handsome white frame high on a hill that looked out into our neighborhood. It was a catbird seat.

"You know, I think we've got the longest sidewalk in the neighborhood," I mused.

"Won't dispute that," Mom said.

"Francis says that our house looks loved in."

Mom took a sudden break from snapping beans. She turned her head slowly to take a good look at me.

"Now isn't that Francis a clever fella."

"Yes, he is," I agreed.

"Now what do you mean...I mean what do you suppose ole Francis meant by that?"

"I don't know exactly, but he also said that you do your work too close by the house. That a body would think you were tied to it by a chain."

"Is that so?"

"Yeah, and he said that it really wouldn't hurt you to come up in the woods some time and play with me...I mean walk around and stuff."

"And stuff?"

"You know, like sittin' by the creek and listen to its soft plunky noises or layin' on the ground and lookin' real close at some of those tiny little flowers I like to pick for you. They're real pretty when you get up close. You only see them after I pick 'em. They've got lots of spunk standing out of the ground."

"Uh huh."

"Or just come up in the mornin' when everything's still wet and the birds are just a chirpin' away like no tomorrow."

"I see."

Mom got up.

"If I did all that, Patti Rae, then who'd make breakfast?"

"I would. I can make scrambled eggs."

"Uh huh. But then who'd make coffee for your father? Who'd wash the dishes and who'd make the beds and sweep the floors and make pretty clothes for you. Hmmm?"

"Yeah, I know, I know. But Francis says that a hundred years from now when we're all dead, that same dirt will be floatin' around keepin' somebody else busy."

"Why that wise old Francis," Mom said with effective sarcasm. "You know he sounds just like your Aunt Rosey, now doesn't he?"

"Uh, not really," I said. Mom looked at me with reproach. "Leastways, I never heard Aunt Rosey say it just like that, really."

"Why she says that every time she comes to visit...just like that or not. She's exactly like you. Wants me to kick up my heels in lawlessness and shirk my duties."

"I never said nothin' about lawlessness."

"You didn't say anything."

"No, and I didn't say anything about shirkin' either."

"Okay. Okay." Mom seemed to be conceding something. "You say it's a bad situation in there?"

"Yes ma'am."

"Then maybe you should go back in and make it two girls."

"I don't count. I'm just Bob's little sister to them."

"Go back in just the same and keep an eye out for me, okay?"

So with a legitimate excuse to return to Bob's feeble party, I did so with a new sense of authority. There I found previously stated matters worse. Mary Lou and Chad were hitting it off to the exclusion of the remaining male occupants causing intolerable behavior. Bob was hitting Bobby Lee over the head with a wood ruler mainly because Bobby Lee was waltzing around the room with an imaginary partner. The point of this was to make fun of Chad. But the point was useless. Chad held on to the only female partner in the room. Once Bobby Lee tried the tapping thing. It didn't work. Mary Lou said "No, thank you" and that was that.

Night descended. Our two lights with yellow tasseled shades were turned on reluctantly and wouldn't have been had Mom not yelled in to Bob.

"Right now!" She insisted.

In this yellow glow of shadowy light, Mary Lou and Chad's slow dancing took on an other-worldly quality. Then, without warning, Mary Lou jumped and screeched.

"Who was that?"

We followed her glance to the south window and saw no one.

"Well, there was someone lookin' in just a second ago," Mary Lou protested.

"Probably Sammy come home from his job at the grocery store." Bobby Lee said and darted outside to see but found only our dog and cat. Mom was in the kitchen washing beans.

"Is Sammy tall and does he have tousled-like hair?" Mary Lou asked and winked at me.

Finally, I was noticed! While I smiled, looking rapturous from this sudden attention, she sashayed over to my side of the room and whispered in my ear.

"Do you think it coulda been Jake?" she asked in her low throaty contralto.

I nodded.

We left, demurely, like Sherlock Holmes and Watson embarking on some secret adventure. Every pair of eyes in the room followed us out the door.

The tool shed was our first guess, then we thought we might find him down by the creek, then relentlessly we searched farther down by the road. I could see Mary Lou wanted to see Jake more than anything, but no Jake materialized. Once back in the kitchen, we remained with Mom. We could hear one of the boys mumbling a sour goodbye and exiting out our front door onto our wooden porch. Clickety clack, clack, clack, clickety, clickety.

"Aunt Martha why do all the boys in this neighborhood wear taps on their shoes? Isn't that hard on the floors?"

Mom's answer was basically ignored. Mary Lou had fallen into another dreamy stare leaving us, once again, in the kitchen by ourselves. Escaping through the haze of romance that filtered Mary Lou's every thought, a slight smile appeared and she gazed sporadically in the direction of the door. This told me something I should have guessed at all along. It was Jake she'd really wanted to dance with that evening. Then she did something I'll never understand. She told my mom.

Instantly, Mom yelled into the living room.

"It's late Bob. Time to get ready for bed!"

I heard Bob announce to his friends that the party was over. There were more mumblings, complaints, tentative plans for the next day's jitney race, a clicking racket on the front porch, then silence. The party was over.

What we hadn't guessed, was that the party was really over. But we wouldn't find out why until the next day.

——— ◆ ———

Later that night, when the hall lights and my little lamp by my bed were out and we could see the stars and the moonlight glinting off telephone wires hopscotching their crescents down the road, Mary Lou jumped out of bed.

"Point out which house is Jake's, would you? Can you see it from here?"

I told her you couldn't and I was glad. It was then we heard the owl that used to hoot in our side yard every night.

"That's Mr. Peabody," I said, smiling, comforted by the fact that although something had seemed amiss that night, most things were still pretty much the same.

"Yeah?" Mary Lou looked out into the dark blue sea of night. "You're so lucky to have a friend like that."

"He's always there. Every night," I said, quite pleased she'd noticed.

"Mr. Peabody." Mary Lou said dreamily. "And don't you have such a great bedroom with matching bed skirt, coverlet and pillow cases?"

I told her she was lucky to be so pretty. I could see she believed me. It was dark, and shadows fell unevenly on her face but there was enough light to reveal a hint of sadness. I wanted to say something to make her feel better but couldn't come up with anything. So I said my prayers out loud to show her I could pray too. Later in bed, pretending sleep, I watched her, fully expecting a prayer or two. But none rushed from her lips like they had the past few days. I wondered for what it was she prayed. Was it to have something so big that it made her cry? If so, her tears were tears of joy. As I watched her from across the room, her face emblazoned with thoughts that were most probably of Jake, I decided to say a prayer for her. After all, this was my very best time with God. During the day, I loved to admire His trees and flowers. But it was in the quiet of my room after my nighttime prayers when Mom knelt with me by my bed summoning Him with her "Dear Heavenly Father," that we talked casually together. This is when I felt Him most, when the world was silent and my heart spoke out in honesty. I wondered sometimes if Mary Lou gave God her quiet times or if they were dedicated only to her dreams. There was no use trying to figure out Mary Lou, it seemed. I would be with her all summer. Perhaps at summer's end I could come to some conclusion. With this thought, I chose to allow my mind to drift.

I imagined the fun we'd have the next day showing her our daffodil fields even though, by now, the yellow blooms had withered and fallen to the ground. And maybe we'd go to the east woods and spot some hobos and then maybe later on in the evening, we'd all climb into our Pontiac and drive fifteen miles down the Ohio River to see the place where dinosaurs once roamed.

Then, with a feeling of regret, I thought about my ballerina doll I'd stashed away in my suitcase the night after our trip to see Mrs. McCullough's moon flowers. I wondered if Mary Lou would like to dress her up. Probably not, and that made me wonder how I would get along the entire summer without playing with my favorite doll. Some day, when she and Mom sat together talking about family, I'd run down to Janey's and we'd dress our dolls and fly them around the world. Or we'd take a train to Chicago where they'd meet handsome men who'd take them to dinner at a nice restaurant with white linen tablecloths. Maybe we'd get them a date closer to home so we could have a more casual hamburger, French fries and a cherry Coke. Janey and I had played together all our lives, and Mom said these were probably our last dolls. But she was wrong. I couldn't imagine not going to all the fun places that belonged only to me and my dear friend.

We still even liked to have tea parties. Janey's mom wrote a poem about us one day after watching us at our tea and polite conversation. She was different from Mom. She suggested we should never stop having tea parties, so we promised her we wouldn't.

I showed my mother Mrs. Green's lines of poetry. I couldn't figure out what the look on her face meant. But she dropped all her chores, I remember, and copied the poem down on the back of a church bulletin. I still have it, written in Mom's flowing hand, tucked carefully in my large volume of Shakespeare:

There's a stump in the middle of our yard where we like to sit and play.
It's a table for our teapot and cups where my friend and I sit all day.
When the sun is hot, it keeps our teapot just right.
Sharing stories and songs in the bright sunlight
Just chatting like our mothers do when they visit each other's homes.
So we pour and sip and chat and we do it all alone,
Except for Miss Bugsy the cat, our beautiful cat.

When the sun has made us tired and we lie on our backs to rest
Miss Bugsy paws at our faces and that is the best.
"Miss Bugsy, stop it!" rings through the woods
Where mockingbirds sing for our neighborhood.
Everyone knows the time by their songs and sweet-throated rhymes.
So when the sun falls behind the hills and we hear the Whippoorwill's trill,
We gather up our teapot and cups and our lovely dresses and hats.
We kiss each other goodbye,
"Bye, Bye!"
And that, as they say, is that.

Suddenly, guilt tugged at my heart. Mary Lou had only just come to visit, and I was dreaming of doing things without her. I wanted to be part of her world, but my own was still redolent of sunny rhymes, the woods' mysteries, sweet simple melodies and make-believe. A glance toward Mary Lou, lying stiffly on my bed, told me she had not yet found sleep. So I watched her watery eyes peering up at the moon that shone like a god and seemed now to move upon her face like quicksilver. I considered the full moon, myself, with its lustrous light and never saw it again without thinking of Mary Lou and how she made that owl mine.

CHAPTER 10

Enchanted Woods

"What's Mary Lou doing down by DeCoursey Creek?" Bobby Lee asked my brother after climbing the steep grassy hill that led up to our house. He and his buddies stood outside our back door looking up at Bob as if he must be insane. A chance to spend time with Mary Lou by the creek! And Bob still in the house? But my brother had just come home from mowing Mrs. McCullough's lawn. He held up the crisp five dollar bill he'd earned. They weren't interested or impressed. So Bob folded it carefully, put it back in his pocket and admitted he didn't know why she was there...not even sure she was. So they went down to the creek to investigate. Years later, Mary Lou told me she thought she'd seen Jake cross over the dam with his eyes looking up at our house that morning. By the time she ran down to meet him, he'd vanished.

It was one of those cloudless deep blue-sky days, full of promise but without any planned events. So, after finding Mary Lou wading in the creek by herself and in a glum mood, my brother and his friends came up with what seemed a bright idea. Crawdads. That's how we ended up chasing miniature lobsters in the early afternoon. Looking back, I remember mostly the sun glinting off the coursing water, its warmth wrapped about me lulling me into an innocent suspicion that winter might never come again. But life is never perfect. Sharp up-turned rocks bruised our feet as we splashed our hands into the sparkling stream missing what darted beneath us. Then there was what we later called, "the creek fight". Sammy and Bobby Lee decided the day wasn't exciting enough. Sammy, having just gotten his fourth paycheck from the grocery store where he carted boxes of product around unpacking and counting, had just purchased a new pair of jeans. I can't remember the label. No one noticed that kind of thing in those days. But there was evidence his mother had just pegged them. They looked tight and stiff. In other words, they fit just right. Sammy was feeling cocky in them too. So Bobby Lee shoved at him to comically illustrate the obvious. Sammy couldn't bend his knees. He fell backward on a sharp rock that tore his shirt. When he cried out, Bobby Lee called him a sissy.

"Well, I'll be a…" It took Sammy only a few minutes, straining at the knees, to stand upright again. We watched the drama unfold as Sammy grabbed the nearest hand-sized stone. "Mom's gonna give it to me when she sees this torn shirt, you lousy…" He threw the metamorphic chunk at Bobby Lee and missed.

"You think you're hot stuff, dontcha?" Bobby Lee couldn't help himself. He ducked and missed Sammy's imprecise fist. "You have to go 'round in that sissy apron lookin' like an old man just to have that stupid job. I wouldn't be caught dead in that apron."

"You jealous son-of-a … my jitney beat yours by a mile!" Sammy looked at those of us who'd witnessed the morning race as if we should confirm his statement. "And you ain't got over it yet."

Bobby Lee took a right jab, then Sammy missed the next punch. Their arms tangled like tree roots and their growls menaced the soft summer noises. It was generally agreed later that the fight was really over Mary Lou.

We moved downstream to let them sort out their egos, a torn shirt, and Sammy's too-tight jeans. Here the rocks, worn by ages of friction, lay more smoothly under deeper water where crawdads were less likely to be found. But it didn't matter. I preferred the cool rushing force of the creek against the calves of my legs. Sometimes the water came quickly up to our knees when we waded out toward the darker, deeper pools. But the creek was still cold from a harsh winter. So it wasn't long before we found ourselves on the grassy banks warming ourselves and dreaming about the coming summer days. I imagined us splashing around in our favorite swimming holes. I'd learned to swim the summer before, first by doggy paddling, then by floating. I couldn't wait to try out my new skill again to see if I still remembered. I'd maybe even swim out to the water that was over my head.

Lying on the thin early summer grass, wondering how one girl could create such excitement, feeling like a third wheel, I kept my mouth shut for the most part and listened to Mary Lou. I admired how securely she answered a barrage of rude questions from Bob and his friends.

She said, "What do you mean, why do I sound like this? You sound just as funny to me probably as I sound to you." The guys looked out the corners of their eyes smiling, secure in the fact that they couldn't sound as funny as Mary Lou. Sammy and Bobby Lee, sullen and quiet, listened suddenly to the conversation. They sat next to each other, now partners in the act of drying their clothes. Then my brother told her she sounded nice.

"I like when you say 'Well, forever more.'" His accent was strained and he craned his neck when he said it which I was sorry for. It seemed too harsh. But we all laughed. She didn't.

Slyly she cooed, "Well, forever more."

I noticed their conversation flowed more naturally there next to the creek than it did when we fidgeted in living rooms or danced in basements. You couldn't lay back on the grass in a living room or pick clover to divert a glance from a thing of beauty too embarrassing to behold for more than a second.

When a conversation about football stalled--Mary Lou didn't know to compliment Chad when he explained a particularly heroic play he'd made last season--and no one seemed to know what else to say, everyone stood up as if some other destination called their names. Only Chad, as it turned out, had any idea as to that destination. Unwilling to give up the barest shred of attention Mary Lou had given him while boasting his athletic skills, Chad told Mary Lou he had something to show her. So we headed toward the woods.

"Here, I'll help pull you up the hill." He grabbed her hand but she wrenched it loose.

"I reckon I got just as good legs as you."

"You ever swung on grapevines?"

She scathed him with a side glance.

"Just asking," he said.

I knew it wasn't a matter of coincidence that I brought up the rear. I wasn't invited officially but, then, no one was telling me to get lost either. So I shadowed the teenagers, running to keep up with their long strides.

Once under the full-leafed canopy, a hitching and bumping of branches high up in the trees seemed a kind of omen. So I watched for some sudden movement or any unusual occurrence in nature once we arrived at the popular precipice where grapevines hung still and inviting just like in the Tarzan movies. Mary Lou didn't look to see if anyone was watching. She didn't even spit in her hands. With a sure grip and surprising agility, she flew out and over the escarpment. Her water-soaked hem flapped in the crystalline air going out. Swinging back in, the wet hem clung to her shapely legs. Instinctively I guessed the fantasy before she squealed it out into the hollow.

"Look! I'm flying!"

We looked…me, my brother, Chad, Sammy, Bud and Bobby Lee. It was her apotheosis. The sheet I'd wrapped ritualistically around her neck–the one Janey and I left in the crook of a tree to use when pretending to be wood fairies–now billowed in the air, mingling with Mary Lou's sundress. Flame-like, her thick, red hair flowed in waves, conjuring up a Thumbelina image in my mind: Thumbelina flying on the back of a Robin. I realize now, many years later, how different my thoughts were from my brother's and his friends. I remember their faces, their eyes. She had them in a daze. They weren't thinking about Thumbelina.

With surprising stamina, Mary Lou held tight to the peeling vine as we continued to push her lithe body past the steep cliff. Counting her now as a daring member of the woods and disappointed a bit in her sudden show of bravery, Bob was busy out-swinging Mary Lou on a companion vine. The farther she swung out from the escarpment, the greater he had to push from a high stump on the hill behind us to ensure his swing would outdo hers. His swings were wider, more dangerous, awkward. Hers were smooth and uninhibited. But in only ten minutes, Mary Lou's hands, unused to these great hanging toys, grew blistered and red.

"Hey, let's show Mary Lou the patch," Chad blurted out. Passing over us on a rock ridge, he had seen her hands. There was sign language behind her back and then a silent group agreement to take her up to the edge of the woods where Mr. Egan's now dying daffodil patch overflowed into his yard like a magic carpet.

"Imagine how bright yellow they are when they're in bloom," I insisted once we reached the western edge of the woods.

"What's that, Patti Rae?"

"The daffodils…you know…in the springtime…close to Easter."

When I saw no emotion, I realized sometimes one just has to see. Or maybe one has to have a mind cleared of all other romantic notions. Jake was Mary Lou's romantic notion that day, so I wasn't surprised that our daffodil patch meant nothing to her. Earlier, climbing toward this green carpet, Chad and Bobby Lee had whispered excitedly as they hung back watching her bounce in her light-as-a-feather trot. It was obvious they talked about her as their eyes glanced her way often, and they smiled curiously at each other in male communion. Then Chad narrowed the distance, throwing intense looks at Mary Lou as he passed her. Once or twice, I saw him side-glance at her until she turned to lock eyes with him. Then he turned to gaze at her straight ahead. I saw it took some guts on his part. She didn't turn away from those looks either. Only shot him that whimsical "Guess what I'm thinking" smile.

We stopped briefly for a break after climbing an especially steep ravine. It was then that Chad, with the careful fingers of a botanist, picked some delicate Blue Bells he found growing next to a fallen rotting tree. Three of their small blooms he arranged somewhat awkwardly, then placed them in Mary Lou's hair. She seemed to admire his sure-footed form as he almost tip-toed toward the mossy stump where she sat broad-shouldered like a goddess. She looked up at him with clear and discerning eyes, accepting nature's ornament with gratitude…surprised, suddenly I think, at Chad's handsomeness.

"You're an angel right here on earth," Chad stated without drama. It occurred to me then, with a sudden change in the wood's light, that Chad had taken some important turn. It was as if some transformation within allowed his heart to speak its mind without fear of what we would say. Years later, our very own Chad made a perfect play as quarterback for Ole Miss. In the halls of that southern university, Chad became an instant hero. But, in my eyes, it was not his college glory that conferred upon him absolute manhood. It was this placing of flowers upon a denied fantasy.

Still, it embarrassed us, especially Bob. When he saw the daffodil patch made no impression on our guest of honor, he suggested something else.

"Oh, come on guys. She hasn't seen our lookout tower yet, and that's about the best thing up here anyways."

Once again we were on the move. The daffodil patch dropped, we made slow progress in the direction of what was really a tree house, some of us taking easier cuts through the gorged-out creek. Bob and Chad grabbed large exposed tree roots to help thrust their bodies upward. They did this with a great show of muscle and grunted to call attention to their strength.

It was an amorphous affair Bob and his friends built four years earlier from cast-off boards they had found in their fathers' basements. Two fat, extended branches held the primitively-made box that was enclosed except for the end that seemed to swallow the nailed-in slats that marched upward from the tree trunk into its mouth. The yawning tree house sat on the highest promontory overlooking a good portion of our neighborhood and beyond. The view of our town from this point was specific to a line of hills leading over to the DeCoursey Yards. We were sitting on the east edge of the tree house, all of us, legs dangling and swinging youthful energy into the cedar air, when we first heard him, then saw him. A man appeared for only a second on the path we'd just taken. He must have seen us then darted into a brake. It wasn't unusual to see other people in the woods. It was just that no adult had ever been known to hide there. Children maybe. Shy children or cautious animals. But no adults. This had been an adult, I felt sure. If Mary Lou had kept her mouth shut, the day may have not made sense. But she blurted it out; maybe she breathed it out. I can't remember.

"Jake!"

The utterance took hope out of the air. I saw its deflating effect. Bob and his friends' shoulder slumped. Mouths grew tight, eyes beady. No one talked for a long time. It might have been for just a minute, but the tension settling heavily on our party strung out the seconds like a taffy pull. Then a branch fell from a tree for some reason. It startled us. The broken interlude seemed to be all Chad needed to speak his mind.

"You know, Mary Lou. You surprise me. A lady like you…"

Mary Lou found no reason to hear him out. She raised her hand as if it was her duty to slap him. But for a mother's call in the distance, she would have. The sound wrapped its arms around her forearm, stopping it mid-air. Ears perked up for some sure identification. Whose name was being called out? Was it Chad's mother? The register of the voice was too high. Another call and we recognized the identifying edge. It was my mother's. It sounded strained and harsh, however, unlike the sing song voice that daily called us to supper.

"Mary Lou! " She cried out again into the echoing chamber of our valley.

"Mary Lou! Come down here right away!"

"Oh, my gosh!" Mary Lou breathed.

Every hand reached out to help her up and then down the primitive slatted stairs. But it was Chad who, making his way to the ground first, took the opportunity to grab her waist, lowering her like a princess to the soft, loamy woods floor.

We were a retreating army charging down steep ravines and rocky crevices, showing Mary Lou the fastest way back. Once at our foyer by the big bear tree, we took different directions. Bob and his friends cut across to Bobby Lee's house. I, not wanting to join in on cooking or sewing that surely Mom must have waiting for our poor guest, decided to find Janey. It was the perfect time for play. The sun was going down behind the hills and her yard would be cool by now, cool enough to play hopscotch or jumping rope.

I was looked at reproachfully when I bounded through Janey's kitchen door out of breath. No, Janey wasn't there, I was informed. Her mother stood over a stew with one of the twins in her arms. She remembered Janey had left an hour before but didn't remember where she said she was going. Over to her uncle's hen house to help him gather up eggs, maybe.

Running full-tilt down their yard and across the highway, I made a dash for the best of the three swinging bridges connecting the west bank to the east bank across our big creek that flowed close by our county road. One step, swing, another step, swing. Jump once, jump twice over lost planking. There was a rhythm to a swinging bridge walk. I left it dancing over the rippling water twenty-five feet below and dashed to the hen house. But no one, not Janey nor Uncle Thurston, did I find gathering up eggs when I looked inside. A lone hen blinked at me before flying off her nest squawking, creating a whirl of feathers that floated out the miniature door onto planking that led down to the ground.

The henhouse was really just another dollhouse to Janey and me. On those days when her uncle went to town, we'd sneak over and make our entrance, much to the dismay of its feathered inhabitants. It was fun to count the eggs and imagine we lived there. That the clucking hens passed us in anger going out as we made our way in, never registered with us. We were too involved in our own fantasies to understand the science of laying eggs even though we'd been warned time and again by her Uncle Thurston calling from across the creek.

"Get outta that henhouse or so help me God I'm comin' over and you'll be sorry when I do! I don't want those hens flyin' round and gettin' upset!"

When I saw that Janey was nowhere near, my mood dampened. Shoulders slumped, I walked back across the bridge that no longer danced but now hung still like my mood. Another day without my friend, I thought as I walked home using the county road.

But my house was where Janey had been all along. I could see her sitting with her ear to my back door as I approached the steep hill that was my yard. I ran like mad toward her when she waved to me in sign language to stop. A bony finger bisected her tense, closed mouth. She was wild-eyed. Slithering away from the door, Janey rushed toward me, grabbed my arm with her wiry fingers, then led me behind our tool shed.

"You're not gonna believe this!" She began.

"What?"

"Jake's the one they think's murdered the woman."

"Huh?"

"I swear," insisted Janey, clinching both of my arms. "I was playin' in your creek lookin' for arrowheads when I heard your mom talkin' real loud to Mary Lou. She'd just come down from outta the woods."

"Yeah? What happened?"

"She told Mary Lou she's not allowed to see Jake any more. Mary Lou said she couldn't make her not see him." Janey gave me a sideways glance. "You didn't tell me they was goin' together."

"They're not! So what…what did Mary Lou say?"

"Yer mom asked her to come inside, and that's when I heard Mary Lou cryin', not hollerin' but kinda raisin' her voice at your mom."

"What do ya think happened?"

"I don't know. But I could hear Mary Lou talkin' loud and oncet I think she stamped her foot. Anyways, I could hear a thud on the floor all the way out here. Your mom told her she oughta get on up the stairs and think about things and that was about thirty minutes ago. Your dad and mom are at your kitchen table right now talkin'."

"Janey!"

It was Janey's mother calling her home for supper four houses over.

"Janey, don't go just yet. We gotta find out what's goin' on."

"But mom's callin' for supper."

"Well, dontcha wanna know if Mary Lou's alright?" I asked but I knew Janey all too well. Nothing mattered to her more than food.

"G'won home," I said.

"Oh." Janey said remembering something. "Your mom and dad kep askin' Mary Lou if she was sure Jake was with you two all day."

I threw a confused look in Janey's direction.

"You know, Patti Rae. The day you two was s'pposed to go to Covington but went to Cincinnati."

"Oh, yeah. I guess they knew all along."

"Mary Lou kep sayin' 'yes.'"

Janey looked at me suspiciously as she held my arms in her bony fingers.

"Was he, Patti Rae? Was he with you all day long?"

I didn't say anything and watched Janey run in her peculiarly smooth, country way down the hill after one more yell from her mother filled our valley.

"Gotta go! Was he?" she yelled back.

131

"Yes," I said but not very convincingly. A hollowness filled my chest.

I crept up to the back screen door. After a few minutes, I only heard bits and pieces, making it difficult to get the gist of my parents' conversation through the trilling and buzzing of insects that increased with the onset of night. Would they make Mary Lou go home? I couldn't tell what it was they said about that. Was Mary Lou being punished by being sent to my bedroom? That wasn't clear either. So I slipped down the yard, then walked up the sidewalk as loudly as I could toward the door. I came in smiling and out of breath. But their deep thoughts made me invisible to them. So I went to the bathroom, washed my hands and face and slipped upstairs without a sound. I found Mary Lou with her head at the foot of my bed taking the full force of the small fan that sat shaking on my dressing table. I could see her sleep was troubled. She turned and moaned and loosely gripped a tear-soaked handkerchief in her left hand. Her eyes were swollen and turmoil still reigned in her face.

That night I slept on the sofa downstairs in the living room. I didn't want the creaking boards beneath my feet to disturb Mary Lou. Just before I dropped off into an exhausted slumber under the south window, it occurred to me that the view of my moon was obscured by an annoying cluster of live oaks.

CHAPTER 11

Jake's Uncle

Morning broke through my dreams earlier than usual. Its intense heat, not the chirping of morning birds, woke me up. Looking out the living room window, I saw that a close haze covered our valley like a smothering injunction. It was too early for dog days, I thought, as I listened to my mother's fretting in the kitchen. Nonetheless, the woods would be unbearable to play in.

"Elliot!" Mom's voice traveled easily through all rooms. "Did you drink the last of the orange juice?"

There was no answer from my dad. Then a banging of pots and pans. Mom's special way of communicating anger.

Mary Lou and I would need to get out of the house as soon as possible. So I began making plans, the central core of which involved Mason's lake and its cool depths into which we would dive and swim. It would be our first real swimming day of the year. Wetting our bodies against the heat in this natural lake, clustered with cattails and lily pads at its southern edge, was one of summer's rituals. It was here we'd catch up on stories and exchange gossip with our neighborhood friends. They'd surely come to the lake on this, our summer's first hot day. We'd loll about on Mason's wood dinghy, the smell of Coppertone wafting through the air like exclamation points. With any luck, Georgia Mason would think to bring her red transistor radio.

Soon, however, I realized there would be no playing or hopes of cooling off by the lake. High-pitched sirens invaded the thick morning quiet. They approached our house from all directions in hysterical clashing of tones. One by one, police cruisers edged up into our yard. Three or four officers from the county and neighboring cities made their way, in slow-paced time, up toward the knot of men already talking in loud protests as they swarmed around my worried-looking father. The police chief from nearby Franklin had brought a few of his own men. It appeared they stayed close to his side in order to underscore his authority. With a considerable belly and hardware hanging like threats from his wide belt, he made the slow ascent up our hill look painful. His young, terse-faced assistants stared straight ahead. They beat Billy clubs into the palms of their hands as if to release egregious tensions.

My nose and cheeks grew hot from the direct sun through the screen window as I watched an unexpected drama unfold. Mary Lou's name piped out from the crowd. It jarred me to complete attention. Dad said she had disappeared…that he couldn't find her anywhere. My chest tightened as I strained to hear and watched my dad under a menacing early heat. It was the first time I'd heard desperation in his usually commanding voice.

"She's striking, not hard to miss," I heard him say.

Striking, not hard to miss I said to myself running mechanically upstairs to my bedroom. I knew the chance she could be hiding in the closet behind my dolls and shoes was a slim one. But I had to find out. She wasn't there. My bed was made, but the room was otherwise in disarray. The suitcase she kept in the corner by my vanity was gone, I noticed, as my heart seemed to fall inside me, racing at the same time. Then I heard Jake's name. It edged its way up through my second-story window in snarls from the lips of those who surely must not know Jake, I thought.

"He's just the type," a thick-muscled brute of a man belted out in an edgey stentorian.

"You can't trust his kind. Never could." Another middle-aged officer added.

"Son-of-a-gun!" an assistant hissed, bruising the palm of his hand with a Billy club after learning Jake was the suspected murderer.

"What's the problem, Officer Moreland?"

"I know Jake. He's one of my brother's friends from school." This was offered by a blond youth who, unlike his seniors, still had slack in his gray police shirt that was carefully tucked in with precise folds. Then he stopped as if some stray thought took him in another direction.

"Go on," my dad urged.

"He...he's not at all what you think he is," he stammered.

A Police Chief took a crack at this remark. "They're all exactly what they look like." He glanced around to make sure everyone was listening. "Punks! All of 'em! And they got an attitude, like they got somethin' on us."

"I'm inclined to think the best of Jake, too, son," my father admitted. The older officers stiffened in a contemptuous manner. "Look," Dad said, dropping his head, "some of us aren't born with equal privileges…"

My father was interrupted.

"I suppose that's right for you, now ain't it?" The Police Chief looked around knowingly, inspiring a few chuckles from his associates. But my father refused to dignify the jab. He ignored him and continued.

"So let's just find him and Mary Lou and then we can ask questions later." My dad's plea was passionate. But I think he must have known that such reasoning fell on pre-determined minds… that he'd congregated a mob, the members of which had already tried and convicted Jake of murder.

Thoughts ran through my head like sands of an hourglass. When I saw my mother passing out coffee to the assembly of scowling men, I made my move.

I grabbed my house shoes and tiptoed downstairs holding them like ammunition. When I left through the front door still wearing pajamas, the sun was nearly at its zenith. Shadows had shortened.

Everything happened in our side yard close by our kitchen door where our land came up to a plateau, creating a perfect setting for Mom's garden. Here, flowering bushes and Adirondack chairs intimated a place of repose. Now in the place of rest, stood eight or ten restless policeman loudly protesting my father's unwillingness to suspect Jake. Smelling their brutal inclinations, I stayed out of their keen sights, slipping cautiously from tree to tree in the direction of the woods to find Francis. I knew if anybody could help Jake, it was Francis.

I didn't have to look far. His short, stout frame filled the bear hole in our big tree just inside the woods. He appeared as one with nature.

"I've been waiting for you," he blurted out in relief.

"You see. You see, now more than ever, Francis!? You've got to come out of the woods. Jake needs your help and you've got to…I know he didn't do it. I just know. And they're…"

"Calm down, Patti Rae."

But I started to cry.

"…and they can't find Mary Lou anywhere," I finished in sobs.

"Where do you think she might have gone?"

I couldn't answer for crying. Francis put his arms around me and waited for me to settle my emotions. I thought he was the kindest, most sensitive friend I'd ever known. And that included my Sunday school teachers who I considered to be high on this kind of list. Hugs were their tools of the trade because, according to their quiet lessons delivered before large posters of Jesus teaching children, Jesus wanted them to love us and hugging was the best way to show it. But with Francis, it was different. I sensed he put his arms around me because he loved me, not because he felt it was his duty. His smile instilled temporary calm.

"I've been thinkin'," I said.

"Yes," Francis looked at me sympathetically.

"I've been thinkin' she probably went to Jake's, but I don't know how she'd know where he lives. I never told her."

"She's been in town for two weeks. Don't you think she figured it out for herself by now?"

"I don't know."

"And why didn't you tell her, Patti Rae?" Francis asked with a look of reproach.

"You know. She was in love with him. I didn't want her to…" but I felt embarrassed to continue.

"You didn't want her to what?"

"…to know how poor he was. I thought maybe Jake could have a dream come true for once in his life."

Francis smiled.

We stood shoulder to shoulder for a moment, our thoughts perhaps bumping down the same road, while a family of robins filled the woods with their exulting tremolos that traveled far distances in the echoing morning air. There was a stand of white pines and Norway spruce just behind Francis' bowed head. Looking up into the limitless blue of a sky that suddenly appeared to have eternal qualities, I became aware of their top branches reaching relentlessly upward in search of their god. To this end, they strove to outdo each other. Shouldering past a competing branch or hitching in swoops against each other from the weight of squirrels. Not so well loved as the robin or finch, a sparrow perched upon one of the branches just above us. I thought how meager was its size and color but, how really sweet its sound and its importance to nature. Jake, I thought. The sparrow's dull plumage gave it near-perfect camouflage against the many-hued browns of the woods. "Fly!" I wanted to say to the sparrow who warbled staccato from its innocent throat. "Don't let them find you! Fly!" I screamed in my mind.

"I know he's not the murderer but I have no proof, just a knowing in my heart," Francis said pushing through my thoughts.

"Me too, Francis. Me too!" I cried once more into his scratchy wool vest that smelled of leather, outside fires and pine trees.

"I'm pretty sure they've got the wrong man pegged, but his hiding out with Mary Lou…it just makes things worse," Francis opined while drawing his beard together with a thick hand. I hoped his knitted brow did not indicate doubt in Jake's direction.

"Well, I'd do just what Jake's doin'," I said taking sides. "He's scared to death! I'd want somebody with me too if I thought people were hunting me!"

"My little funny face. You don't understand."

And I didn't as I watched Francis pound a fallen branch into pieces with his right foot.

"Francis, can't you just come down and tell 'em what a good boy Jake is? You could tell 'em how you watch over him sometimes when his Dad's in a drunken rage. How you stand outside his house just in case he needs you. And how he never does 'cause he's smart enough to take a walk or back off until his Dad's passed out. You could tell 'em how many times you've seen Jake carry his Dad, gentle as a lamb, outta Babcock's saloon with everybody tauntin' him to leave his Dad to die on the road. You could do that, couldn't you Francis? They just need somebody to get 'em to see."

"Patricia," Francis began with something that seemed would be reassurance. "Do you think people would understand what all that might indicate?"

I blinked.

"Why," he continued "would these policemen whose sole desire in this life is to get ahead, provide homes and food for their children…men whose busy jobs give them little time…why would they take time to understand what's really in the heart of one man when people all around are convincing them to think in only one way?"

"But you understand, Francis," I said, looking up now with hope that he could tell me something different.

"But I am not as worried with my home and things I have no control over. I live mostly up here." I thought he would indicate, with a sweep of his hand, the lush woods that now seemed to lean in just a bit for its compliment. But Francis only pointed to the frontal lobe of his brain. "No, Patti Rae. People who live outside the deeper region of their minds rely on set ideas provided by someone else. We all suffer from this. Not just our policemen."

Wise old Francis scrutinized my face to see if his point had been well taken.

"You're making excuses!" I shouted.

His raised eyebrows dropped.

Then slowly his hoary head shook from one side to the other with just a hint of a tragic smile like the fabled Ulysses after his life-changing voyage. But there was no satisfaction in me.

"So what is in the deepest part of our brain that no one seems to use?" I thought I might trip him up. I waited for what lengthened into an eternity. He seemed to chew a cud that suddenly grew into his mouth. His eyes, enlarged and unblinking with what appeared to indicate a chain of ideas, gazed into an unfamiliar ether. His breathing shallow, body inert, Francis seemed to write an epitaph in the gathering gloom. And then, without even as much as the usual intake of air, he whispered:

"It is the part of us that connects with God."

I waited for more, for something that would indicate Francis could help. Only just five hundred feet below our yard, the men, appearing small from our high view, were thinking desperate thoughts and spewing vile words. They were most definitely connecting to some inner part of their brain but it bore no resemblance to the region just described by Francis. As if reading my mind, he said,

"They wouldn't like it, you know, if I, a stranger, came out of the woods."

What I thought he meant was that most men don't like to be told what to do by other men especially if they're an outsider. Dad told me that once and I figured Francis probably understood this too.

"But you wouldn't have to worry, Francis. You're not a stranger, really. Mom and Dad know you're my best friend. They suspect you're my imaginary friend, but if they could just see you, they'd remember all the wonderful things you've told me." I rubbed my tears away with a pajama sleeve. "Dad said, whoever you are, he'd be honored to make your acquaintance."

"Well, I'd like to meet your Dad some day. There's no doubt about that. He's about the only man in this town I'd like to meet but…"

I pleaded with my eyes that were now blinking tears away and squinting from the direct sun behind him.

"But today's definitely not the day," Francis sighed.

"Why not? Why not? It's the best day. I mean Jake really needs you and I know you like Jake a lot. I thought with everything you told me, you'd do anything for Jake. I thought that was your way. I thought…"

"I've got to stay up here and watch everything. That's what I'm best at, Patti Rae."

"Well, you can stay up here all you like!" It wasn't what I wanted to say. What I really wanted to say was that he was a coward. "But I'm not gonna stay up here. You can bet that. I'm gonna…oh never mind!"

And I left his side without blurting out the hateful words crowding upon my tongue, sobbing as I ran down the hill. Francis didn't yell after me and, for that, I was disappointed. If only he'd apologized or admitted he'd like to help but couldn't because he would have been a suspect, something that would have made sense to me. Later, I wondered how long he stayed at the edge of our woods just watching. Did he disappear into the heart of the woods or did he climb up that 200 year-old tree to get a broader view of our neighborhood and the officers whose fear and anger ran through it like a plains fire? And I wondered, more than anything, if he stayed long enough to see Jake's uncle.

A persistent buzz of alternate plans seemed to take shape under our tall live oaks. Then, one by one, police cruisers that had pulled up into our property's first terrace, sped off in different directions. As I came down from the woods, I noticed old man Babcock snooping about to make sure no one had left tire ruts in our yard. As he walked back, satisfied no damage had been done, I ran inside our hot kitchen.

"Oh, for goodness sakes, Patti Rae!" Mom rushed toward me anxiously. "Where in the world have you been?! We don't need two of you missing!"

I apologized quickly so Mom could tell me what had happened early that morning.

She cleared her throat.

"Well, your dad got up early to get a drink and noticed the back door wasn't pulled to. He went upstairs and saw Mary Lou was gone, but he was relieved to find you sleeping in the living room. Then he went up by the woods to see if she'd taken an early morning stroll. But soon he put two and two together. So he woke me up and we drove on down to Jake's. Lands! You shoulda seen the inside of that place!" Mom looked up to the ceiling as if she could see through it to the sky. "Jake's mother, who I haven't seen since God-knows-when, she said Mary Lou had knocked on their door around five o'clock this morning. She said Jake left with her but didn't say where they were goin'. She wasn't in the habit of asking Jake his whereabouts since Jake's a big boy and makes his own way in the world. Of all the…But I do feel bad about chastising her," Mom admitted tenuously biting the end of our wooden spoon used to whip up scrambled eggs. "I shoulda just kept quiet."

"Do the police think they know where they are?" I asked.

"No, but they won't be leavin' any stones unturned today. We've just got to say our prayers, that's all."

I agreed. Turning to make a run upstairs to dress, I thought I glimpsed movement outside our kitchen door. The movement turned out to be a man who looked as though he meant to knock but seemed shy and unsure of himself. He was short and stout, much like Francis. I'd seen him before but couldn't remember where. I slammed the door behind me.

"Hello," I said. Are you lookin' for my dad?"

"No," the gray bearded man, who now I realized looked almost exactly like Francis, said in a quiet voice. Then he whispered.

"I'm lookin' for little Patti Rae."

My shoulders shot up in good posture.

"Well you got 'er. What can I do for ya?"

"Jake and Mary Lou asked me to tell ya somethin'," he said scratching his beard and looking nervously at our kitchen door out of which cooking sounds clanged ominously.

"Really?!" I said, excited, but he put his hand on my arm and said he didn't want 'nobody' to see him.

I showed him behind our biggest sycamore and he explained, with a uniquely native intelligence, what had happened.

"Ya see, Jakie...I call 'em Jakie. He's my nephew, ya know. And by the way, ain't you growed up."

Then I remembered who this Francis look-alike was. When I was seven years old, I fell off old man Babcock's rock wall and hurt myself trying to balance three scoops of ice cream that leaned dangerously in a small sugar cone. Jake's uncle came out of Babcock's saloon smelling of strong drink. When he heard my crying and saw my friends teasing and laughing at me, he rushed over to my side and whisked me off the ground with his short stout arms. With a strong Appalachian accent, he reminded them--and Janey was one of them I hate to say--that I was their friend and that it was sure a pretty day when your own friends laugh at you. Their high-pitched cackling shut off like water from a tap. I remember how they looked away from his accusing eyes but stood their ground as much from fear as stupid shock. He wheeled away from their muteness with me in his arms. Just before we entered Babcock's, Janey yelled.

"I'm tellin' your mom you're in the saloon! You're gonna get in trouble, Patti Rae!"

But at that point, I really didn't care. Sharp pains were shooting through my leg.

The inside of Babcock's was dark with colorful lights strung like tinsel above the bar. Red stools in front of the long bar spun unwillingly if you pushed them. The gentle man sat me on one of these stools while a frowning Mr.

Babcock brought a dampened towel. Together, they cleaned and bandaged my knee. Then Jake's uncle and I sat at a table where he told me all about the mugs on the shelves above the bar and how they came from Germany. He explained, in his curious way of talking, that my friends were just young and that when you're young you're "more mean" but that when you get older, you, for some reason, become nicer. He said that doesn't always happen. But what I noticed is that he was so sincere. While I inhaled a surprisingly tasty hamburger cooked up from Babcock's black-encrusted grill, this leprechaun of a man talked endlessly, it seemed, to calm me down. Meanwhile, Mr. Babcock had called my mother. She appeared timidly at the saloon door just after I'd finished my last bite.

"Mom!" I yelled toward her.

She rushed through the door, her face tight and anxious. It was strange to see her in a place of drink, surrounded by men who looked at her in a curious way. But they were invisible to her as she thanked Jake's uncle so profusely that I thought she might even bow besides shaking his hand. She called him a Good Samaritan which put the idea in my head that he was the very man we read about in the Bible. To this kindness, he added a hug. Then he placed a shiny nickel in my hand so carefully, I thought it must be gold. I never spent it and still had it in my top drawer where I kept special things. I wondered how it was I'd almost forgotten about him because for a long time, I could see his face whenever I was in trouble. I had imagined he would come and take care of me no matter what. I looked for him again and again without success. My vigil lasted for about three months or so. Eventually, I forgot about him. And now this! My Good Samaritan finally showed up again and could not have chosen a better time!

"Ya see, Jakie," he continued, "he's a good boy. Good to his mom. Good to his ole man."

He cleared his throat while I watched the sun-etched lines carved into his face in a warm feeling of reunion.

"Why, Jakie never killed nobody. That day he left you and your purty cousin, all he did was he jest had to get home 'cause he tol' my sister, his ma, he had somethin' special for her. It was her birthday, see. She had lunch on the table close near an hour when he finally got home about one-thirty. And, sure 'nough. Jakie had got her a pot a African valets—never forgets his ma's birthday," he stressed with a turn-down of his head. "But that's how they spotted him."

I blinked my eyes not quite following.

"They saw 'em at Tater's Bait Shop just above the railroad yards buyin' those African valets that Tater keeps in the back mostly for hisself. But he likes Jakie. Well, most do who knows him good. And so Jakie, he had to go back a the shop and get 'em hisself. Got my sis the biggest one he had about yea big..." Jake's uncle indicated a large African violet with his soiled and broken hands. "... and that's when they caught sight a him. His boots tramped through some mud and I guess they thought he done it 'cause the lady was found in a muddy spot jest close down thar by DeCoursey Rail Yards, and it was about that time a day they figger she got murdered. And they said Jakie looked nervous and in a hurry. But Jakie wouldn't hurt a flea. Not a flea! And then your ma and pa asked Mary Lou yesterdie if Jakie had been with her all day over in Cincinnata. When she said he shore had, then they got s'picious 'cause they knowed he was seen that day 'round that hour at Tater's. And Tater's so close to the Yards 'n all. And, well, it's not lookin' too good for Jakie, 'specially now that your cousin's done run off with 'em."

I thought about the roses that day. The careful way they'd been wrapped and that satin white bow that encircled their innocence. I could still smell the fragrance that had been for Jake's mother. But it was Mary Lou who took them greedily, who made assumptions that comes with privilege. I thought about how Jake's finances must have been depleted after this extravagant purchase and then there were our treats on the ice cream bridge. There'd only been just enough money left over to buy his mother some African violets. Tears filled my eyes with desperation and ran down my cheeks as love for Jake, but mostly fear, consumed me all at once. I thought about how any other young man would have forgotten his mother's birthday. It must have been a tense day for Jake. Meeting Mary Lou, wanting to become part of some once-in-a-lifetime love, his mother at home waiting for her devoted son to share in a birthday lunch...a birthday no doubt seldom remembered by her drunken husband. And now everybody thinking Jake was the murderer!

Suddenly my mother stuck her head out the door.

"Patti Rae! You come on in for..."

But it was too late. She caught sight of Jake's uncle who had been migrating up the hill as he talked, away from the protecting tree.

"I guess I'd best be gettin' on," he said dropping his head. "But the thing they wanted me to tell you is, is that they want you to bring 'em Mary Lou's change purse. She said it's in the suitcase inside yer closet. You know the closet she's talkin' 'bout?"

I nodded my head.

"It's got extra money in it and they need the money purty bad now. You know what she's talkin' bout?"

I nodded my head again.

"Now don't tell a soul, ya hear? They're over yonder at Mason's barn, clar up in the hayloft."

"I'll take it over right away. I promise." I beamed at my Good Samaritan.

Inside I could hear Mom on the phone.

"...and hurry!" She said.

"Mom!" I yelled. Now, feeling that Jake's uncle could vouch for his nephew, I ran to the screen door. "I got somebody who can explain everything." But Mom wasn't in the kitchen.

When I wheeled around, Jake's uncle was also gone, which was good. I'd already forgotten my promise to keep all this to myself. Mom had gone upstairs for something. I could hear her rummaging around. Cereal and fruit waited for me at a lonely breakfast table, so I sat down in an anxious state eating everything quickly in ravenous gulps.

It was a funny thing seeing mom with Dad's shotgun. Mom hated guns.

"Whatcha doin' with Dad's gun?" I asked as I peeled a banana.

"Nothing," Mom demurred placing it, like fine crystal, in the hallway as if she'd changed her mind about something or had more pressing things to do. She picked up the skillet and utensils on the stove and began washing them in our double porcelain sink.

"You seen Francis lately?" Mom asked. It wasn't like Mom to bring up Francis' name. But I thought it was nice of her to inquire about my best friend.

"Yeah. I saw him just today."

Mom's eyebrows lifted. Then she did something unusual. She sat down next to me with all her chores in limbo.

"Does Francis still have his beard?"

"Yes ma'am."

"He's short? Is that what you told me one time?"

"He's short and has a short neck and is built like Uncle Mosby. Good ole Uncle Mosby. Hows come we never see good ole…"

"Did you talk to him much today?"

"Yeah. We always talk a lot."

Mom gave a sigh, but she got closer to me the way she always did when trying to get a good look at my tonsils.

"Has he ever said anything about the lady who got murdered?"

"Yeah."

Silence. Then.

"What did he…"

There was a knock on the kitchen door. My heart bounced with high hopes. Jake's uncle had come back to explain everything to Mom! He would make everything right!

But it wasn't Jake's uncle. Three policemen with their shiny billed hats glinting sun through the screen and into our eyes stood looking away from the door out of courtesy.

Mom went out and led them away from the door. I heard her say "Thanks for coming." A few minutes later she yelled. "Patti Rae!"

"Yes ma'am," I said getting up cautiously from the table.

"You wanna come out here. These gentlemen would like to talk to you."

"Hello." I said smiling as I slammed the door behind me. It bounced two or three times before settling down. Then I noticed Harley.

"Hi, Harley."

"Good afternoon, Miss Patti Rae."

"D'ya ever find Dillinger's money?" I asked, noticing immediately that it didn't seem a topic close to his heart at the moment. Harley was the friendliest cop who'd ever patrolled Jefferson. He liked kids and, when on his breaks, would regale us with chilling stories while sitting in Babcock's parking lot. Our favorite story involved John Dillinger and how the old road that followed the railroad yards had been one of his best-kept secret hiding places. He encouraged us always to be on the lookout for hidden boxes in our woods just west of this country road. It was there Dillinger was believed to have buried his money. But now I could see Harley was in no mood, or maybe he was just too self-conscious, to discuss this kind of thing.

"Your mother says you have a friend in the woods," the oldest of the three officers directed his comment to me drawing up a forced smile.

"Yeah!" I said thinking that maybe now people were beginning to believe me.

"Where do you normally see your friend? Francis is his name?"

"Yes sir. Francis sure is his name and he's about as nice a guy as you're ever gonna meet."

"Really? Why is that?"

"'Cause he has time to listen to all my stories. I'm surprised Harley here hasn't told you about 'im. Harley knows him pretty good."

The other officers looked at Harley who seemed ill at ease again, so I decided to make things easier for him.

"Yeah, Harley knows him 'cause I tell him about Francis all the time. Right Harley?"

Harley gave the faintest nod.

"Ol' Francis never says anything bad about nobody and he seems to always have things figured out."

The questioning officer looked at the others and smiled.

"What is it that he has figured out?"

I scratched my head and suddenly felt an urge to use the bathroom.

"Well, he knows mostly what's in people's minds."

"He's a mind reader?"

"Not exactly. It's more like he knows what's in people's hearts. That's it. You know..." I continued warming to my own voice. "...he usually always knows why Mom's upset."

Now mom was recoiling. I wondered how this could embarrass her but decided there was no use asking. I changed the subject.

"Like for instance, he'd say you three men are just doin' your job and that people are only scared of ya because we all have guilt feelings goin' on some of the time."

"Did he ever say that…in those exact words?"

"Why, yeah! He did as a matter a fact. He said policemen are our friends and it helps if you wave to 'em like they're real people. He said you get tired of being run from. That's what he said once."

"And does your friend ever run from anybody?"

"Not as far as I know. He just never seems to be around when I want him to meet my friends. I think he's kinda shy. You know what I mean? Like Mrs. Hutchen's daughter who never comes out 'cept to get on the school bus. Some people are just plain shy."

I started to tell them how glad I was that I wasn't shy and that I could speak my mind. At least that's what Dad always said. But Mom gave me a look. She was good at keeping this kind of talk to a minimum. For some reason, she found it necessary to advise me on a frequent basis that I should avoid talking about myself. Always talk about things or other people, she would say. It was a hard pill for me to swallow because, in those days, I considered myself a fascinating subject.

"Did he talk to you today about the murder?"

"Yeah," I said with my voice pitching high. "He said you guys have figured wrong on Jake. Jake wouldn't hurt a fly. He knows it and I know it."

The other men shuffled a bit and looked like they wanted to take off.

"Does he ever talk about your mother in a familiar way?"

I looked at Mom.

"What do you mean?"

"I mean does he ever say he'd like to meet your mother?"

"Yes sir. I think he did say that once. But I'd been askin' him to come down outta the woods and make her acquaintance. He said he'd just rather watch her from afar. See, he can see her cookin' most times through those windows." I pointed to our boathouse windows that faced the ever-patient shade of our woods. "And he usually always knows when we're gettin' ready to eat. Sometimes I wonder if anybody ever cooks for him."

"What is Francis' last name?"

"Well that's funny you ask 'cause I've often wondered about that myself. I figured since he lives up on Hickory Branch Hill Road that it doesn't matter, really."

"What do you mean by that?" The third officer chimed in.

"Well, I figured he's just Francis from Hickory Branch Hill Road. Ain't that good enough?"

"Patti Rae!" Mom propped her arms on her hips.

"I mean, isn't that good enough?"

"Your Mom said you were talking to him today."

"Yeah!" I said. "He's probably up there right now. I can take you up if you like. He's real good at hidin', but I figure if I beg him to come and meet you, that you need real bad to talk to 'im, he'll come out for sure!" I was all smiles but nobody else was smiling.

"Does he have special hiding places, Patti Rae?"

"Oh, yeah. Francis is a great hider."

But suddenly there was a nod to Mom and the officers headed up for the woods.

"Hey!" I yelled. "Don't you want me to come along?!"

"You stay right there with your mother. We'll be back, Patti Rae."

I looked at Mom who sat on our rock wall. She wiped the palms of her hands on her apron, a nervous gesture that confused me.

"Why are those men all of a sudden interested in sweet old Francis?" I asked, noticing their unsure footing as they entered the woods, following age-old worn Indian paths that generations of kids had kept beaten down. Then suddenly a thought occurred to me.

"Oh, Mom. I know. They're worried about him. They think he's in danger with a murderer loose and all. But they don't have to worry..."

A torturous look on my mother's face told me things weren't just right. As I watched the last officer follow the others into our woods, I noticed his hand reaching into the holster of his belt. It took him only a half second to cock his gun.

"Mom! They better be careful and not shoot Francis by accident. Now that would be a cryin' shame, wouldn't it? Trying to protect him and then havin' an accident."

"Yes, it would, Patti Rae."

"Well, ol' Francis. You don't have to worry about him. He knows everything that goes on in those woods and if he sees somebody comin' at him with a gun, he'll…" It started in my shaking stomach and came up in a gasp and then tears. It took me a while to sort through reality arriving at a vague truth that shook my usually strong eleven-year old constitution. My emotions took over from there. Mom grabbed me around my head and pulled me to her. I could feel her trembling. Suddenly we heard the officers yelling, echoing out of the vastness of our now dark and brooding woods.

"Hey, Buddy!! Stop right there!!"

The shots cracked up through the tall canopy of trees numbing me down to my toes. My crying stopped long enough to listen. Then Mom said something that stopped my breathing.

"Oh Lordy, Patti Rae. I think they may have got 'im."

"Got 'im? Got who?" I still didn't want to believe the obvious.

With a sigh then a whisper she uttered, "Francis."

"Francis? I don't think…"

First there was a slight movement near the path, then Harley came lumbering out of the woods straight down to us. His frightened barn-owl eyes told us the worst.

"I'm sorry, Miss Patti Rae. I'm so sorry. I never thought your old friend Francis was really up there. I swear I didn't…" Tears fell from his eyes freely and without shame… "But he ran from us and had a gun and Officer Bartley got him. I just had to come down right away and tell you how sorry I am. But…"

He paused when he saw my confusion, desperation…my hatred for the man who shot Francis.

"Patti Rae. I didn't mean for this to happen. I swear!"

I stood like a dumb wall with emotions coming out of every crevice. Francis had been shot? Why? Why would Harley let them shoot dear sweet old Francis?

"Why, Mom?" I asked sobbing and moving away from her. "Why? Why did you let 'em do it? My friend. They killed my very best friend!"

"Patti Rae, he could be the murderer. He could have been playing with your mind all this time and..."

"Now sweetheart," Harley chimed in. "He was probably just settin' you up."

"But I told you all about him. I told you how good..."

But there was, it occurred to me, nothing more to be said...nothing worth saying. My best friend had been shot and for what? Why would someone shoot the nicest man in the world? Why, after my confiding over and over all of his little wisdoms, as my father called them, would they think he was the murderer?

"Patti Rae! Now you come back here! He just told you all those nice things to fool you!" Mom's strained her voice the farther away I ran.

Then Harley's voice broke in: "He was just lyin', Patti Rae! Some people just lie to get what they want!"

Harley may as well have been a Shawnee loosing arrows through the thick oxygen-poor air of lost innocence. THWACK! THWACK! THWACK! They pierced my tense young back as I ran.

CHAPTER 12

Francis' Retreat

Crows cawing in the distance. Concentrating on their sound. My heart pounding frantically.

My thoughts ran in a direct line…sucking in air with gulps and coughs to stave off shock. I continued my flight, crossing Mason's field after detouring from the road into a copse past Mason's long, steep gravel drive. Then, fording a shallow part of the creek, cautiously I slipped through a line of cedars, then out to the field and toward the barn.

I have always taken barns to be playhouses, great wooden caverns as much suited to children as to animals. That day, I approached it like a haven. After sliding the barn's wide door to one side with surprising strength, it stopped me: Mary Lou's Evening in Paris cologne. It came to me like a burst of lavender paint against the brown and black palette and fertile smells of the slate-shadowed interior. By memory, I walked past the first set of feeding troughs, tripped clumsily over a tin bucket, then reached for the loft ladder. Damp and rough to the touch, I took each step deliberately, loudly whispering: "Mary Lou! Jake!"

Nothing.

"Are you there? It's me. Patti Rae."

A short powerful puff of breath issued from one of Mason's well-fed Jerseys. Listening closely but hearing only multiple chewings of cud and heavy pawing of hooves, I became doubtful.

A brief look around, my eyes adjusting to the darkness, told me Mary Lou and Jake were gone. After searching every corner of the familiar hayloft, I discovered their nest within a mound of high hay. Probably they had decided they were too near the road and had taken off for the east woods. But where in the woods would they have gone?

It seemed a good idea to simply wait for their return or for a better idea. But the hours sat on me like a concrete block. Through the cracks in the barn's wall, I watched the strips of yellow sunlight grow dim. Surely they would come back for the money, which I'd have to tell them I'd get later. Right then I needed something from them more than they needed money. I wanted to tell them that Francis--the thought ran through me like ice and my skin tightened into goose bumps--I had to tell them Francis had been shot, maybe killed. They had killed my Francis. Dear God, they had killed my Francis!

In the dark vastness that seemed now to belong only to me and Mason's cows, I gave into the inexorable pressure that had built up like steam in my throat and chest. With every sob beginning in my stomach, bursting out in great waves of coughs then long squeals of pain, I spewed out emotions of shock, disappointment, then some indefinable hatred. Overriding all was a deep longing to see Francis again.

I'm not sure how long I cried within this great hall of grief, but it must have made the Jerseys sorrowful for they began to low. It was enough to make my crying stop at once. Their calls might bring old man Mason down with his lantern in search of a fox or some menacing critter. So, without the outlet of weeping, I shook. A surprisingly cool dusk dampened the night air that blew through a high window. I was still in my thin pajamas.

By some kind providence, I found Mr. Mason's old raincoat that hung from a nail by the high window that spilled hay to the outside. Mould lay in its outside folds from lack of use. But the inside was quilted and felt good against my skin as I shuffled around in search of Mary Lou and Jake's nest once more.

As I waited, twisting and turning in the hay, I felt a dull pain in my chest, and my haunting sorrow gave way to intermittent short quakes and starts. Without knowing how tired I was and with the barn's great familiar cloak of darkness upon me and a security that Mary Lou and Jake would surely return, I must have slipped into some vague form of sleep.

It seemed I was unconscious like this for only seconds when I heard him call my name.

"Patti Rae."

"I'm up here!" I yelled feebly. Suddenly I was crying again. Whether it was from a desperate lonliness or some primal need to share my grief, I didn't know. Then the dark image appeared at the door and his husky cough reverberated against the barn walls. When I realized it was Francis, time stopped. My heart surged with joy, and as suddenly as they had begun, my cries abruptly froze. I moved closer to the ledge of the hayloft to better peer into a face that I loved. Directly beneath me, the full moon shed its silvery light through the high window above the door and revealed Francis more clearly. He was in pain.

"Up here!" My voice quivered so violently, I scarcely recognized it.

Francis, always sure and quick, found the ladder and came up with little trouble. Clearing the top of the ladder like a lion on the ledge of a mountain after a tiring hunt, his body relaxed and, with pathetic relief, fell into a smaller mound of hay that must have seemed like heaven to him. The darkening blood from his badly shot arm flowed down his shirt, then into rivulets between the matted straw.

"Oh, Francis! They didn't kill you. They…"

"Please, Patti Rae. Don't cry. Help me off with my shirt. I'm going to use it as a tourniquet." He faced me in excruciating pain. "Here, help me."

"Sure, Francis." I continued to sob and found the buttonholes through blurring tears. "We've got to get you to a Doctor."

"No. That won't be necessary."

"Why not?"

"Because…" He winced and so did I. Suddenly it was as if his pain were mine.

"Because," he continued, tearing strips from his shirt for bandages. "… because they now believe me to be the murderer. I ran from them. It's all they needed to see."

"But, Francis, it doesn't matter. You're hurt and you'll bleed to death if we don't get you to a doctor! I'll make sure nothing happens to you. Dad will help us. I know he will."

"You still don't understand."

"What don't I understand, Francis?"

"It doesn't matter now. I'll stay here with you until Mary Lou and Jake come back."

And he did, and I never questioned how he knew I was waiting for them. But that was his way. He always knew and understood the great ebb and flow of my life. With some misgivings, I watched him fall into what seemed a dangerously deep sleep, the thick air of sweet-smelling hay lingering heavy upon us. A stray moonbeam from the northwest window moved upon his face like a nursery rhyme. So I sang to him one I knew, thinking it consolation.

Sing a song of sixpence,
A pocket full of rye.
Four and twenty blackbirds
Baked in a pie.
When the pie was opened,
The birds began to sing.
Wasn't that a funny gift
To set before the king?

Still and calm, his face reminded me of Mrs. McCullough's moonflowers. His pale complexion appeared slightly moist and, somehow, beneath its surface came a preternatural shine. I thought of Mary Lou and how she approached the moonflowers that night. It was the underglow of the flowers' skin that held her back, I think, as if human touch would disincline their heavenly reach. Through a veil of near sleep, Francis smiled, laid his wide, thick hand on mine in his usual protective way. As always, it gave me an ineffable sense of love that I think he always knew I needed most.

More than anything, peace reigned in his unwrinkled brow. It was a brow I'd recently watched closely, for it revealed to me, in some basic way, his inner turmoil and most pressing desires. But now I saw peace. How strange when peace, at this moment, seemed so elusive. But there it was, a mysterious glowing, like a falling star. I cradled his head. I caressed my childhood guardian angel. Now I was his protector.

"Patti Rae!"

———— ◆ ————

They stood over me in the darkness. The moon's new position gave them partial sillouhette.

"Mary Lou!" I jumped up from my sleep. Damp hay clung to my face as I wrapped my arms around her. Mary Lou was all right, and suddenly I felt an intense kind of love that comes with a sense of near loss.

Jake looked unimaginably cheerful. Beaming with a proprietary arm around Mary Lou, he put his hand on my back.

"Don't cry, funny face. You don't need to cry anymore. Nobody killed your Francis. That was all a big misunderstanding."

I lifted my eyes, straining to separate my dreams from their silhouettes. In the semi-darkness, I saw they were smiling. But I continued shaking, my tears seeming an endless river. Jake, in his black attire that now seemed almost priest-like, knelt beside my quaking body and took me in his long arms. Mary Lou knelt down also and took us both in her arms. There was an anxious pause…of tears being pushed back by both Mary Lou and Jake. I'll never forget the unity of our emotions.

"They caught the murderer, Patti Rae! No one's huntin' Jake now. Everything's all right." This incredible utterance in Mary Lou's undying southern drawl still burnishes my memory of that moment. Suddenly the heavy smell of hay became a smell of delight, of complete and utter happiness.

"They have? They aren't?" My crying ceased instantly. I looked down to tell Francis but realized they might not have seen him yet. Quickly, I averted their attention not wanting to give him away. "They found the murderer?" I asked again.

Mary Lou nodded, smiling, beaming.

"We heard you singin' in your sleep, Patti Rae." Mary Lou put her hand under my chin now that I appeared calm.

I remember how warm their bodies felt next to mine, how from this very proximity I drew hope where there had been what it seemed the longest desperation for the affirmation that touch brings.

"What was it you were singin'?" she asked.

But it was just too much. There in the almost religious safety of the barn, the need to reach down for Francis was greater than my restraint. To take his warm strong hand, to hug him, to make him part of our fellowship. To tell him that he and Jake were no longer suspects. Should I awaken him just to give him this good news and assuage his fears? It seemed the only thing to do. I turned quickly, not thinking about his aversion to people, his preference to only me. But it didn't matter. He was already gone.

"Patti Rae?" Mary Lou looked in the direction of my gaze, then back at me. Surprisingly, it took me only a few moments to recover.

"I was singin' a song to Janey. You know, my friend Janey?"

Mary Lou once again looked down to where my gaze had fallen. "Yes, I know. You were singin' a lullaby," she said with curious empathy.

"Yeah. I dreamt we were sayin' goodbye 'cause we were both getting married and I was goin' down to Dixie and she was goin' up north to her aunt's. Her aunt was letting her get married in that big house Janey always talks about. Anyways, I felt real sad that we wouldn't be seein' each other any more so I thought I'd sing her a song. A goodbye song."

"Well, now, that must'a been a fine dream," Mary Lou admitted drawing stray hair away from my eyes.

It was one o'clock in the morning when we climbed down the barn ladder and walked under a full moon toward the flashing red and white lights. All the commotion was over at Janey's Uncle Thurston's. They'd found the murderer in the hen house.

As we walked holding hands, me between Mary Lou and Jake, they sporadically lifted me off my feet, so exhilarated were they by their improved fortune. On our way to Thurston Pile's hen house, I learned all I needed to know of the day's events and how the murderer was discovered.

It all began with a young and ambitious police officer who decided to follow his instincts. He'd read a bulletin two days before about a one Jonathan

Lorre. This unfortunate forty-five year-old patient had escaped, in a rage, the premises of Forest View Hospital, a Cincinnati insane asylum. When young officer Hayden interviewed the Director of the hospital, he asked why there seemed to be lack of concern for Mr. Lorre. The answer was given in a simple but direct manner. Mr. Lorre had no known relatives but they had accepted him into the asylum anyway. "Then," the Director explained with little emotion, being busy with over sixty-five patients and family members milling about, "he left as simply as he arrived."

Officer Hayden, armed with the suspect's description, followed the escapee's route from one hole of a restaurant and boarding house to another where Mr. Lorre had begged for food. Obliquely following the line of rail from Cincinnati, over the river and into Kentucky, the policeman had caught the scent of his trail. It had been relatively easy. Everyone remembered him. Emotional, jumpy and evasive when asked questions, he had created suspicion. At one railroad boarding house, he'd even washed dishes for a week to pay for his expenses, breaking several glasses and plates during this interval. He left his mess without a word after being cruelly chastised by the owner's wife. In only two days, a collection of grim stories and an occasional good tip on Mr. Lorre's whereabouts led young Hayden ultimately to Thurston Pile's henhouse. He found Lorre sitting with the hens around nine o'clock that night, dirty and delirious, nearly starved and in dire need of medication.

Earlier that afternoon, Jake's uncle had waited at the edge of our woods to watch me leave with Mary Lou's purse in hand. He wanted to make sure I carried through on my promise. Then the somber-looking police had shown up. So, he waited even longer to see what transpired. Unfortunately, he waited too long. As he watched the officers approach the woods, he thought nothing of it. When they took the path he was on, he could hear them discussing the looks of the murderer. It was a perfect description of him. Realizing it was he they were pursuing, Jake's uncle employed the use of a large stick to beat down thickets through which he knew the officers wouldn't follow. He outran them even after one of their shots caught him in his right thigh. When Mary Lou and Jake saw him dragging his leg, edging toward the barn in the distance, they ran to help him to the road. Mary Lou and Jake hitchhiked the wounded to the hospital without thought of their pursuers and against the protests of Jake's uncle. While they were in the emergency room, they heard the astonishing news: The murderer had been found.

Mary Lou had memorized our telephone number by heart—Hemlock 1-0772. So she called Mom from the hospital telephone booth to apologize. She let my mother know she was all right and that Jake's uncle had been shot behind our house in the woods and was being tended to by an emergency room doctor. After a moment of crying and relief, my mother told them what happened after they had heard the shots: "Patti Rae was beside herself! She ran away because she thought they'd shot Francis! But I guess it was Jake's uncle. Who woulda guessed?"

They'd been looking for me for hours. But Mary Lou and Jake knew where to find me. They convinced my mother of this as she drove them back from the hospital. She dropped them off at the top of Mason's old country road, and they had guessed right. They guessed I'd be waiting for them in the hayloft. What they didn't know was that Francis had been with me for the very last time. I would never tell them it was to him I sang that song.

CHAPTER 13

Lost Paradise

It was a small crowd. Had the hour been later or earlier, everyone from our neighborhood would have shown up. In the quiet cluster of about thirty people, all of whom I recognized, Jonathon Lorre was the frightened animal of a human being lying center stage upon the grass. His grimy handcuffed hands lay in his lap when they weren't flailing around like some moon-ravaged Werewolf. Up to this point, I hadn't believed in Werewolves. That night I decided such creatures go over much better on television accompanied by bright commercials and a corny master of ceremony like our Ghost Host on local TV. There in the flashing lights, the heavily-bearded man appeared not only frightening, but tragic in a way that made my stomach pitch.

Just about everyone from that end of town was there. Pumping her wirey legs, Janey was a bright bobber in a small subdued pond of humanity. In front of her, a protective line of teenagers, arms held tightly in an intertwining row, made a kind of barricade. Her older brother insisted she go home but his efforts were futile. Bob and Buddy Lee chomped on large wads of bubble gum, blowing them out into iridescent globes of pink. When Janey saw the three of us come down from the road, she darted off in our direction. She clutched my arm and drew me toward the scene. I remember the cold dampness of her hands.

The four of us found a chink in the circle of adults and police officers through which we could view the perpetrator responsible for all our recent miseries. A short man in a white coat attended upon the highly excited Mr. Lorre. My mother tried, without success, to feed him soup she'd brought down from our kitchen. We gasped when he bit the spoon with his snarling mouth flinging it at her. She stood bravely, I thought. Mr. Babcock stood behind her, hands on her shoulders, protesting her efforts.

"It's no use, Martha. It's no use."

My mother was no fool. She knew her attempts to feed him only skimmed the surface of his needs. But it was what she had to offer…her domestic gift of love. When the ambulance arrived, blocks of people moved in unison allowing the various hues of colored light to move surprisingly like liquid with a haunting cast.

Janey's parents, in great solemnity, appeared suddenly out of the darkness like two saints of peace. Janey's mother, mountain tall and broad of shoulder, took Janey in her strong arms and comforted her by smoothing her hair and patting her small back.

"You shouldn't be down here, baby," her mother said. "But I guess you've see'd it all by now."

Suddenly, with Janey contented to bask in the security of her mother's arms, I was left to my thoughts of relief and feelings of deep change.

Mary Lou and Jake held hands in the damp night air, the combination of cruiser lights and flashlights flickering upon their smiling faces. Admiring their matched beauty of love and some understanding of the universe and how they found their finite place within that huge reality, I couldn't have imagined a better pairing of two souls. I really can't imagine now, so many years later. Even so, my eleven-year old intuition suspected that their souls could be divided by less honorable forces. Or perhaps that was something Francis had put in my mind. At that time, I wasn't really sure. The more indelible image of that night was that this ordeal had brought them closer together. They were smiling, in a perception of acceptance, and I found it strange that they should seem warmed by trite apologies that some officers offered in hollow voices. But no apologies issued from our neighbors who, I now realize, may have been disappointed with the night's outcome. Starcrossed lovers would have made a better story. It would have made those people herded about, whose relationships, grown dull and unimaginative with each passing year, seem not so bad.

The overripe eagerness that had pitted Mary Lou so ecstatically against this very world, appeared now to recede before my eyes. Her jaw, set not so tight or high as in the past, seemed currently occupied with some struggling survival of a diminished ancestral dignity. But still they smiled. Mary Lou and Jake. They thought they'd been redeemed. For just that night, they had.

It took four men to lift the murderer into the ambulance and a host of us, listening to the animal cries of Mr. Lorre, to spend a lifetime forgetting that crazed sound. One by one, each man representing the law, sped off in his cruiser taking with him guns, Billy clubs and flashlights, emergency props that had created a temporary shock theatre for our small town.

Then, bereft of sirens and showy members of authority, we became aware that some of the townspeople still loitered about the henhouse. Strange behavior caught our attention. From across the creek, we could see grown men squeezing their large frames through the small coop door; others stood outside peering into the small windows. One man pointed to an exact spot, respectfully explaining to an old-timer, telling him, no doubt, exactly where the sick murderer had been found. Mr. Shortcakes strutted noisily around and flared his wings at the few who dared disrupt his perfectly-timed sleep.

The three of us were drawn by the curious few whose ghostly conversations echoed tentatively from across the creek. So we walked lightly over the swinging bridge in order to take a look at the scene ourselves. The group of teenagers, now without entertainment but revved up by the arcane events, formed a dance line behind us. Bobbing and swaying, arms linked, they sang a popular song by a young new artist out of Memphis--Elvis Presley. He was a controversial pop star their parents agreed would never last.

The warden threw a party in the county jail.
The prison band was there and they began to wail.
The band was jumpin' and the joint began to swing.
You should-'ve heart those knocked-out jailbirds sing.
Let's rock..........

I remember being surprised at this outburst, as I assumed the adults would have preferred a more somber ritual of loss. But I've learned since then that teenagers see their lives in immortal terms. It gives them that positive slant which wise adults turn to for future hope. That pitch black morning, their ability to celebrate the joy of community despite a somber event, overshadowed the deep solemnity of their parents who saw only the tragedy.

By the time we trudged up to my and Janey's imaginary playhouse, Mr. Truthers, crouching beneath the low ceiling, had taken it upon himself to give the small house of chickens a thorough going over. He found one empty tuna can, a stick that had been used as an eating utensil, and some pop bottles buried under dirty straw. The female victim's necklace had been taken by the police in evidence of murder, we were informed. Then, through one small window toward the back of the hen house, we watched Mr. Truthers pull something long and sheer out of the corner. Its bright color contrasted sharply with the tarp the murderer had apparently used for warmth on chilly nights. Setting my mind more intently upon this object, it soon came to me what it was. Its length and significance gagged my voice. It was Mary Lou's nylon scarf, pink with white polka-dots. As our neighbor brushed the dirt and straw from its length, my mind went back to Mary Lou's second day with us when we were dressing and the small pebbles peppered my screen window. *I'm outside the window, not inside. I watch the scarf drop from her delicate hand. In slow motion, I see it curl and twine upon the air.* Was it one of Mary Lou's dreams, an illusion or an ideal love she gave this scarf up to in sacrifice? *I'm now back inside the room. I remember her giggle and look of rapture as we remain pinned to the floor, waiting for a call or some response from the new owner of her pink scarf.* It never came.

The early morning temperature continued to drop. It was either that or the shock of seeing her scarf that made Mary Lou shake. Mr. Truthers looked carefully at the pink sheer nylon, guessing it had been the deceased victim's. Neither Mary Lou nor I told anyone it was hers. Her hand came up to her mouth, and I watched her grow dizzy with each shallow, quick-paced breath.

Her world, like mine, had changed forever.

An innocent illusion of her flaming youth, some bright star in the solar system she felt only she had seen and could reach, fell suddenly underfoot. It was only one of her dreams, but it had been trampled too soon and too dishonorably.

CHAPTER 14

Found

A s I sit – in my mind – beneath Gilbert's old shade tree down by the big creek where the banks are wide, I contemplate my return to this parcel of earth and this flowing water after so many years.

Now that my reconstruction of dear old Francis is complete, I clearly see he was a manifestation of a luxury that children no longer seem to have. Sweet, empty time. Time for creativity. Time for imagination. With that incredible childhood advantage, he became as real to me as the paternal sheltering of our woods and hills. He was my ultimate security, like the miles of woods I played under, my leafy blanket of protection. But I realize without question, as I listen to the trickling enticement of this creek, so was the water.

Meandering through the land of my childhood was this insistent creek that flowed and still flows into the Licking River, a larger river that meets the Ohio River in roiling communion. It rolled on softly, year after year, cooling our overheated bodies through those heady summer days as we grew to be admirers of nature's beauties and smells without even knowing it.

When I left its embrace, it all fell away. Like leaves from an autumn tree, yearly shedding food for next spring's birth, the wisdom of nature became perennially invisible to me. How was it that I lost sight of its continuous cycle of protection? Too busy? Too many false worlds to conquer? Too many high and important-looking buildings in the way?

It is clear to me, however, that Mary Lou never lost sight. She did what she said she would do. She married a small-town lawyer and lived her life out in the country, rearing two fine boys who shared her love of horses, trebling creeks, and her contagious happy anticipation. By slow degrees, I came to understand that indescribable attribute that seemed so unique to Mary Lou. It was quite simple, really. She loved herself so well that it led her to love others with the same degree of intensity and, perhaps, purpose. Ultimately, we all look for our own pathway to God. This was Mary Lou's.

I suspect Jake never stopped loving the intoxication of Mary Lou's self-love or whatever it was that kept him dreaming past expired hopes. Jake was Mary Lou's early dream grounded in the highest star in her skyward vision. But Mary Lou was Jake's shimmering dream that went beyond any star she could chase.

In 1969, I came home for a brief period just after college. On one particularly clear day, heavy with the smell of honeysuckles and wild roses, I found myself at Jake's old gas station. Filling my battered Corvair at a self-service tank, I lamented the recent loss of full-service convenience. I remembered the narrow black cord that rang for the service attendants inside during the fifties, as the wheels of cars pressed upon it, rolling to a stop under the wide awning. It was a minor remembrance but it was enough. Standing alone and with no cars pulling in or out to interrupt my thoughts, I walked back in time through the tricky haze of the past. I was eleven years old again, and I watched as a young willowy Jake came kindly toward me with his present of candy. I leaned out the window of my parents' car, smiling up at him. My mother sat at the wheel in her smart gray hat and matching gloves. Rifling through her purse, she found the few dollars it would take to pay for gas and the service of filling our old Pontiac.

As suddenly as this vision appeared, it vanished. But it had turned my inner eye backward. I considered the yellow-brick canopied filling station building so uniquely engineered for a different era. I couldn't resist the temptation to go inside. Would the candy jar still be there? It wasn't. But the old swing door with a bay area window still sat on its spring-loaded hinges. I was told Jake had "got his own station" years ago. Not being far from the address given me, I drove nine blocks north on Madison just to gaze upon the gentle blue-eyed boy who'd once stolen my cousin's heart.

"Jake!" his young assistant barked under a car that seemed to have enveloped its mechanic leaving only two long legs sprawling. I could tell Jake might have hugged me had he not been covered with dirt and grease. Yes, he remembered me. How could he forget, was his remark. "Still got those dimples, I see."

I blushed, but not with my head down in my shoulders as I used to as a child. My red face was a thanks and I smiled.

He yelled back to a tall, broad-shouldered employee who knelt tediously over a tire re-treading machine. One shoulder buckle from his coveralls had broken loose. "Aint she pretty?"

The large man smiled broadly, nodding. His tired eyes sparkled suddenly. Jake added with sureness: "It runs in the family." His manners were as impeccable as ever. "How's your mom and dad?"

"They're doin' fine, Jake."

"I'm still in love with that cousin of yours, ya know. But that's just between you and me." And he winked, then narrowly grinned a meaning to me I'll never forget.

As I drove away, I imagined he might tell the story about Mary Lou one more time to his burly workman who would faithfully listen. There were pictures of children on the wall in Jake's office but I had made no comment. I just wanted to see Jake. I didn't want the story of Jake beyond Mary Lou. I was still young and naive enough to think that certain things in life should stay constant for memory's sake. So I didn't ask Jake about his wife or his children. I should have. But it was clear that my asking was unnecessary. Jake looked happy.

When Mom died in 1989, Chad came up from Atlanta to be with us. Showing us pictures of his wife and five boys, he reminisced, relating a story particularly close to his heart. When his own mother fell ill just about the time he entered his senior year in high school, he remembered our mother bringing hot meals in every day for him and his dad.

"She didn't like us fussing over her and told us we didn't have to thank her every time she came over. She said it was her neighborly duty." His voice broke.

After the funeral, Bob, Chad, and I drove to Mitchell's Big Boy in a sudden mood to visit some past remnant of our happy days together. I think we could all still see the white and black-checkered floor, the silver money changers attached to waitresses' belts, the white pocket hats held secure by bobby pins. It was a plain-clothed waitress who led us to our table and asked for our orders. We crowded into a booth shouldering each other as if, by physicality, we could turn back time. We made no comment when we were told they no longer had Cherry Cokes. We devoured our hamburgers and French fries without guilt. It was then Chad confided his feelings about our youth: We'd all been spoiled…not just by our mothers but by life. Where did all that free time go to, he wondered.

"No one sits on front porch swings anymore."

Now I see that this recent reconstitution of my childhood days was as much about Francis as it was about my enchantress cousin, Mary Lou. Francis, a wonderful concoction of Dad, Gilbert, old man Babcock, Jake's uncle, maybe some of those tired, wayfaring strangers who used to come through town like ghosts from the Depression. For the most part, Francis was the precocious part of me that yearned for the ideal. Life was simple and slow enough for me, back then, to hold this ideal up for hours and gaze upon its face.

I've met maybe one or two Francis' in my life but never felt compelled to feel any particular empathy or desire for a man like him who, I learned early in my life, could be so loathsome to the herd, whose goodness and kindness equals weakness in this world. But then, by the time I met those people, a hard shell had formed around me…a hard shiny material made of rugged individualism less humanity. Now I seek him out.

Francis, are you still there?

It is a miracle of life that when we seek beauty, it comes to us. John Keats had it partially summed up when he said: "Beauty is truth, truth beauty". But how vacuous is beauty without love? So, with these recent memories of Francis, I've amended his observation: Truth is beauty, beauty is love, love is the essence of life.

Listening to its soft rushing as I imagine sitting by my old creek, I wonder if perhaps the water's deepest mystery is where it might take a wise person even beyond the golden days of childhood. Following it by boat or by some humbler means, it rushes us past playfields, past refineries, then past the commercial skyline that industry creates; but then on further to the wider expanse of untouched trees and hills, pure and limited only by the improvements "civilized" man places upon it.

The great distiller of atoms, the quenching basin of life, I want to dip my head into its mercurial stream. Now that I've revisited childhood memories, perhaps at some point, I'll do just that. I'll come up for air with new eyes that show me, in genuine terms, the humanity we are all meant to share and protect. It is the least I can do.

About the Author

Ellen Everman was born at Covington's historic Booth Hospital which sits at the edge of the Ohio River. Free to roam the woods with other Baby Boomers, she grew up in the once prim valley town of Fairview just south of Latonia, a Northern Kentucky city. She attended public schools and gradu-

ated with honors from the University of Cincinnati receiving her Bachelor of Arts Degree in English in 1981. She has contributed both fiction and non-fiction articles in various publications, among them Arts Across Kentucky, The Sunday Challenger and the Kentucky Post. She has travelled extensively throughout the country and abroad observing varying cultures and dialects. Tennis, dance, guitar, painting, reading are her hobbies. Drawing from her collection of short stories written mostly about her youth, Ms. Everman has created this fictional novel that paints a vivid and unforgetta-

Photo by Douglas Rowe

ble picture of the border town area known as Northern Kentucky/Cincinnati. Visit the author at www.pinkdicenovel.com.